Winter with the Cliff Dwellers
Book One in the Prophecy of Peace

First Edition

Published by The Nazca Plains Corporation
Las Vegas, Nevada
2007

ISBN: 978-1-934625-44-6

Published by

The Nazca Plains Corporation ®
4640 Paradise Rd, Suite 141
Las Vegas NV 89109-8000

PUBLISHER'S NOTE
Winter with the Cliff Dwellers is a work of fiction created wholly by *Jamie
E. Laleff's* imagination. All characters are fictional and any resemblance
to any persons living or deceased is purely by accident. No portion of
this book reflects any real person or events.

Cover, William Walsh
Art Director, Blake Stephens

Dedication

My sons, who inspired me,
May your futures be filled with adventure!

Acknowledgements

I would not be a good daughter if I did not start off by thanking my mother, the first person to tell me "I really, really like it." You kept me going.

I most importantly want to thank Jean M. Auel. Your work taught me that sometimes passion and imagery are necessary in order to remind us what it means to be human.

I would also like to thank Bryan Kolar. You once told me to follow my dreams. I did, and it flowed out of my fingertips like ink from a pen. This story has grown beyond anything I could have predicted and it never would have been told if not for you.

In addition, I would like to thank all the Fantasy and Fiction Authors out there that came before me. I can only hope to live up to that which you have already accomplished. May my future readers enjoy my work as much as I have enjoyed yours.

Before I am completely done, there are countless Architects and Authors who have filled my mind over the past decade. I dream of building my own home such as one finds within due to the progressive (regressive) work of extraordinary American Architects.

Winter with the Cliff Dwellers
Book One in the Prophecy of Peace

First Edition

Jamie E. Laleff

Contents

Introduction

Please allow me to draw you a picture of a very small world. I want you to hold up your hand and imagine it a bowl made of clay. Open your fingers a little and see how the years have worn away at the rim. Cracks and chips produce a very irregular pattern. Now fill half of the bowl with sand and dip the opposite side into some water. As the water seeps threw the cracks and begins to swirl in the sand, filling this small world; look around it anew, and see as I do....

To the north, the mountains rise high above the sand, forming the most rugged, yet beautiful, terrain ones eyes have ever seen, as dense forests cover the rocky slopes. Beyond lies a mighty glacier, the likes of which no man has ever survived a crossing and returned to tell about. This land is known as the land of the Cliff Dwellers. Home to the wealthiest people and mightiest warriors known to this small world. Their ruler is the widowed Sorceress of the Wind, Jacqueline; mother to three fine princes. All of which are worthy of following in their fathers' line.

To the east, you see the High Dessert reaching south between fertile fields that crowd every river and stream to cross the most expansive Land of the Plains. Home to farmers, hunters and herders... This is where you find the widowed King Kerill; father to two strapping young lads who lead their people in the most humble lifestyle of worshiping the Earth, which once granted their late mother strength as the finest Sorceress of the Earth that their small world has ever known.

As you begin to look south, the land and the sea become one as trees and hills emerge from as murky a swamp as one would see in their worst nightmare. Such a land as this is filled with the mysterious People of the Mist and is ruled by a most greedy King Jaredoe, absent father to one son and one daughter. Our vantage point allows us sight of the rising mountains far inland, revealing the mineral rich deposits held sacred by hidden artisans. Outlanders rarely see anything beyond the first inland road before being caught by the many groups of highly trained guards, scattered between villages through out this inhospitable land, at King Jaredoe's command.

As the land slowly gives way, you are forced to look back to the west once again. Following an ever growing chain of islands, you eventually find yourself on the greatest island; home to Queen Thema, the Sorceress of Fire who resides on the southern side of the island. Her one and only child, a son, born the bastard of a Cliffman Trader, now resides within his Uncles care. Her son is in hopes of proving his worth upon the Sea, by following his Fathers lead; as many of his cousins have before him. For the islands are known for their fruitful forests that provide enough to harvest and trade almost all year long. As prince, he will have his own ship, once he proves he is of age to take the lead as captain.

The one thing that unites these four lands is the sea. That which allows trade to prosper... and yet, also that which threatens the peace. For in this small world, we have four known lands and five known races of people... The Cliff Dwellers... The Plains People.... The People of the Mist... The Islanders.... and The Seafarers... The last of which have survived countless generations of homelessness by maintaining the traditions of their ancestors. Once known as the finest map makers, these masters of the sea began charting the most fruitful soil, and began planting the most bountiful crops. Said crops are still harvested to this day by these mysterious foreigners who come ashore by moonlight.

Though cultures vary greatly, these fives races share one gift granted by the stars. As much a blessing as a curse, each race carries within its' blood the ability to utter its own words. This gift can only be passed between mortal man and mortal woman threw passion and desire. Though many have attempted to learn the tongue of a foreign land, not much is ever clear to the native ear without the slightest hint of affection. A gift must be bestowed upon the lips of a foreigner before their words can clearly be heard.

And thus, I leave you, as a pure and humble Plainsmaiden awakens within the hull of a Seafaring ship...

Chapter One
The First Day and Night

The first sounds she heard were that of shouts and clashing metal in the distance. Men were fighting, and dying, not far away. The wooden floor beneath was rocking her so violently, it could only mean she was at sea, but where? She tasted blood in her mouth; this made it clear that she was not a willing passenger. Pain shot through her ribs and pounded in the back of her head, this told her she had to be a fighter. But who was she anyway? What was her name? More importantly, why did she find herself bound and gagged in the dark?

These questions would run though her mind unyielding. Fear only stayed itself so long as she heard the battle beyond. 'Stay away,' she prayed, not knowing who would be the victor and who had been her captor.

With some struggle and even more pain, she was eventually able to turn around in the belly of the ship. Daylight glinted between planks of wood above her. In the shadows lay barrels of varying sizes, piles of furs and a mound of fabric. Some bags were stacked beside her that looked to be filled with flour. Leaning forward with all her might, a wave helped to push her up. She held her balance just long enough to fall, rump first, onto the stack of bags. Through a knothole in the planks that must have been the deck, she could see clouds growing darker. 'Oh for some rain...'

She had not thought of her thirst before now, 'How long has it been since I last had a drink of water?'

Falling into darkness again, she did not notice the growing silence. Somewhere in the distance, the battle had been won.

"I want a full list of their cargo as soon as that ship is brought into the shallows. That storm grows more fearsome by the moment. We will all be sleeping far up river tonight. Have some of the men begin making camp on the other side of that bluff," said the Prince.

"Yes sir, shall we bring the goods ashore?" was the only question to his orders.

"Only that which you deem perishable."

"Of course." 'What a silly question to bother him with,' he thought as he stepped into the rowboat headed out to the ship. 'Prince Cirtap is only so patient after a hearty beating. Although those thieving Seafarers probably deserved it!'

Countless tales had reached their shores of Seafarers raiding unprotected coasts. Word had it that they had even begun rowing up river in the dead of night only to surprise unsuspecting farmers far to the south where the land grew flat and fertile.

'What bounty had they gathered on this trip?' he thought as he approached the vacant ship. 'Could not have been much for Merrick to give up the fight so easily.'

He climbed up to the deck to see evidence of how unprepared for battle they truly were. Primo, as the royal family called him, saw not a single thing on the main deck, not even the standard water barrel. As he walked down the stairs into the galley, he counted no less than fifteen long swords and seven daggers still sheathed in the far corner. The real treasures would be found through the next door, so he waved a couple men to guard the door before he kicked it open. As their eyes adjusted to the dark, Primo stepped into the cargo hold to see something the likes of which he had never seen before.

"Get the Prince, he'll want to see this for himself."

Rather annoyed at the thought of being summoned to look at a cargo hold, Cirtap ordered his men put their backs into it and row at double time. He wanted to be back ashore before the rain began to fall.

"What on all the Earth and Sea could deem me coming out here Primo?"

"Below, Sir!"

Now he was curious. 'Below, just below...' So below he went.

The galley was already empty of all but a table and a few chairs, so he opened the door to the cargo hold. At first glance he saw a pile of furs, 'nice catch,' some jugs of liquor and water, as well as some fabric from the plains. He heard a moan, 'My men would never let the pains of battle be known!'

Then he saw her. In the shadows, a pile of no less than four hundred pounds of flour was holding up a young woman. 'That might be why some showed fatigue early in the fight.'

Please understand that a female hostage taken forcefully was not uncommon, but not only was she not much to look at (normally Raiders took the most beautiful of women), she was still dressed. To make matters all the more intriguing, she was dressed in such finely woven white cotton that no person could mistake her as a simple farm girl. And oh how they had beaten her good. Only a woman that screamed all night would end up gagged. Her bare arms were badly bruised and her bare feet were still muddy.

Yet for all that, her long bountiful skirts were still intact! The Plainsmaiden cords of purity still bound the fabric tightly to her, all the way from her breast to her thighs on either side of her body. Astonishing to think what this girl had gone through. Why had she fought so? By the look of the blood oozing down the side of her head, she would soon die for the fight.

'If she is meant to live, I will help,' thought the prince.

As the men began to gather behind him in the dark shadows of the cargo hold, he waved them to silence and pulled his short blade from his belt. 'Will she wake? Will she run?' Cirtap lifted the bottom edge of her skirt and slipped the cold blade between her ankles to cut the ropes bound about them, just as she began to open her big brown eyes for the first time and looked down at him. He quickly moved to her wrists only to feel her hands wrap around his. He looked in her eyes and saw fear staring back. With a flip of his wrist, her hands were free and Cirtap slipped the blade back in his belt before untying the gag about her head.

She licked her chapped lips and looked around as fear pounded through her veins. Several large men were crowded into the hull by now. Most all of them were so tall as to barely be able to stand below the deck while their upper bodies were so muscular that not a single one of them could let their arms fall to the side. Much like the man at her feet, they all had wavy black hair, they all wore fur vests that were covered in blood, and all of whom were starring at her.

The man with the knife reached to one of the men standing behind him, then offered her a bladder of fresh water. He was such a large man that he gladly knelt before her within the hull of the ship as he helped her to drink. Even with fresh blood on the shoulder of his leather vest, he still smiled when he put the bladder to her lips.

How very good it felt pouring down her throat. So cool and clear, as if from a magical stream. Such a drink had nothing to do with this place as the smell of rotting fish overwhelmed the senses. She took another long drink as he stood up and began speaking.

Now she knew she was far from home. None of the sounds coming from his mouth formed pictures in her mind.

"Send the row boat with word for my mother," Cirtap told Primo. "This girl will need all the help we can give her. We'll take her up river to the camp sight in this ship. I'll await my mother in the great tent. And Primo, tell the men to hurry, the storm grows near."

Before she could find her voice or think of a single word to say, he bent down and slipped one massive arm under her legs. His other arm was then slipped under her ribs.

"Ah!" the pain made her cry out, ever so slightly, as light faded dark again.

The girl sunk into his arms as Cirtap lifted her unconscious body up to his chest. He held her safe in his arms like a sick child, until he laid her on the bunk within the captain's chamber, for what little remained of her voyage.

Night had fallen by the time she woke again. Now she found herself surrounded by heavy tarps tied from pole to pole forming a large circle. Several poles formed a tight circle in the nearly flat roof, just off center, where a fire still glowed. The fire was just large enough to light the enclosure, and bringing a surprising amount of warmth. Directly below the opening in the roof, next to the flames, sat a large metal bowl collecting rainwater, it had several cups hanging on the sides (obviously for drinking). In the far side of the enclosure hung some fabric. She could just make out the form of a pot near the bottom of the curtain. The only other inhabitant of this great shelter was the man that had cut her bonds, still wearing the bloody vest and leather leggings with his sword touching the ground at his side.

'I must have passed out,' she thought, 'He must have carried me here.'

Unlike before, he now looked extremely tired. He slept where he sat with his head leaning on his arm propped on a table near what must have been the door.

'I must keep quiet so as not to wake him, he looks so tired.'

With fists and teeth clenched she rose to find her ribs had been tightly bound. Her dress lay on the floor and all that covered her was a very large shirt, obviously cut for a man.

'I hope this man is a healer,' was her next thought.

If not for the furs laid upon her, her hips and legs were fully unclad. This fact would have brought fear to her if not for the hunger pains growing in her stomach. Her first attempt at walking landed her firmly on the floor as her twisted ankle shot pain up her body. So crawl she must to relieve her water.

Cirtap, awakened by her fall, watched through cracked eyelids to see for himself what mysteries she held. An extreme amount of pain could be readily seen though her shaking muscles as she struggled to the far pot (not knowing one was beside her bed). Her thighs of smooth hairless white shimmered in the firelight revealing the sinew of a warrior rarely seen on women, let alone a girl. He had already guessed her at fourteen springs, not yet a woman (at least no womanly curves to speak of). Yet a fighter none the less.

After using the pot, she returned to the fire where she added some small sticks, enough for a quick flame and than a newer log. 'She can build a fire, interesting,' he thought.

Next she found a comb. By the new firelight, she released a bundle of hair at the back of her head and proceeded to comb out all the knots incurred during her time at sea. Once her surprisingly long hair was recoiled, she washed her face and drank some tea, 'She also knows some herbs, mother will be pleased to know that!' Finally, she grabbed a wheat bread roll beside her bed, lay down, closed her eyes and ate a meager supper with only half the fur upon her.

When Cirtap was thoroughly convinced the girl slept soundly again he rose to put things back in their places. None but his mother would know of her strength. With two broken ribs, a twisted ankle, fractured wrist, concussion and countless bruises, she still made it twenty paces to let her water before preparing her own tea and tending her bountiful hair! Clearly she would live through the night and then some. Something gave him a feeling of peace as his bare feet wiped her tracks off the floor. Though his mother had been kept off the coast road by the downpour raging outside, some healer had found their way to her. No amount of bandages could bring such a return in strength. She would live and the storm would pass. The sun would rise soon and it would be a glorious day.

Chapter Two
Queen Jacqueline

Morning brought a wagon carrying the queen down the river via an inland road. Traveling by night had been cold and rough. The Queen, however, knew it must be worth it. Her youngest son would not have sent for her, unless it was extremely important. The Queen's entourage arrived at the camp just as the sun broke the horizon.

A familiar sight she had not known for many years lay before her. This sheltered meadow allowed for a great tent to be surrounded by no less than ten tents worthy of housing four warriors each. Lean-tos had not yet been erected near the river for work stations and none of the cooking pits had yet been lit, instead they sat coldly holding puddles of water. She instructed her women to work as quietly and quickly as peace would allow. She wanted fires built and lit with tea brewing before any but the head guards awakened. The Queen even had the wagons stop some two hundred paces from the camp, as she wanted the horses to graze without disturbing the sleepers beyond. As unheard of as it sounded, the Queen would walk the rest of the way through the camp alone. She would waste no time with formalities this morning as her vision quest the night before had been blocked by an unknown force. Something powerful was afoot and she needed to learn why immediately.

Silently the Queen crept into the great tent. Her son, the greatest warrior known to her men since his father, lay helplessly sleeping by the door. Across the fire upon a raised bed (normally reserved for her alone) lay a girl. Curiosity stayed her temper for the moment as silently she crept over to what had once been her bed. Upon closer examination the queen saw bandages upon the child. She had been bound as a warrior in need of healing about the head, chest, arm and foot. 'How can this be? No child is permitted on a battlefield.'

Clearly by the look of her son, the messengers were accurate in that Prince Cirtap had slaughtered a band of raiders. By daylight, their blood could still be seen upon his clothes. Even his sword had yet to be properly cleaned. Yet here was this girl!

"Let me look into the eyes that would bewitch my son," the Queen said as she leaned in closely. 'That face, as if a memory, is so familiar.' But memories are no longer what they once were. 'Dreams will bring back the memories I need. For now, I will let her live. Fate would not allow me to see her in the truest of light if she were not blessed. I just wish I knew by who,' she thought as she lifted the fur to cover the girl once again. Then, she turned around and smiled at her big baby just beginning to drool on the table. "Cirtap. Cirtap, awaken my son"

"Yes mother," murmured a sleepy voice. "You have arrived? You must be famished from you journey, let me get a servant to bring you some tea," he said as he started to rise.

"There is no need. It will come when it is ready. My women are already at work so that your men can sleep. Now, tell me how this child comes to lay upon my bed," commanded the Queen in her most motherly voice.

Day after day the Queen sat by the girl's bedside. Only Queen Jacqueline knew of the herbs she mixed into the tea. Some for healing, some for strength and some more for sleep. But most especially, a drop of the Queen's special mixture to guide her dreams. For alone at night she would watch the girl toss in fit-full dreams. Her dreams were strong, strong enough to remember. And remember she must, for only through her memories could the truth of her existence be known. Somewhere, another sorcerer or sorceress had bonded with this child; good or bad, that bond needed to be strengthened. Only in sleep was this possible. Soon her sons Selrach and Rewdan would return from their voyage of peaceful trade with the neighboring land of the Plains. If the child would be persuaded to loosen her tongue with Rewdan, the queen would soon know all.

Insisting the child was still weak after nearly half a moon's rest, Queen Jacqueline sent her son Cirtap, with several hunters, to gather fresh meat from Green Valley. The first snow would be falling soon and the camp was primly located for catching the herds coming down off the mountains. Many more of her people had already begun to fill the sheltered valley between camp and the ocean shore. Soon they would hold the festival of the first snowfall. Now, more than ever, she needed the girl to remain within the tent, as she had become a secret pet of the queen's. Only the most trusted of maids knew of her existence. That is how the queen had insisted it be from the first onset of this mystery. Only Queen Jacqueline knew that her bandages were no longer needed. Yet sleep she must, within the seclusion of the great tent, until the Queen knew she could trust the foreigner.

At long last, a ship arrived bearing Prince Rewdan. Her first born son Selrach was no where to be seen, but this was not a surprise to the queen. He could easily be returning upon another trade ship within a few more days.

"Greetings mother, sadly, bad tidings I bring on such short growing days," Rewdan said upon finally walking into the camp. "My brother Selrach is lost to us."

"What tales could cause you to bring such tidings to me? My son remains in good standing and I will not hear of any treachery against my blood." The Queen was obviously distressed. She had sent her three would-be Kings into the world carrying a small glass vile of her own blood crafted within their swords that she might know of their faring at all times. They could not fall unless their sword had been removed from their hand. So strong was her craft that no mortal man could merely strike down the bloodline of Jacqueline. Yet how could it be that he sends no word? Not by land, or by sea. "We have much to speak of

Rewdan; I want to know every detail." She turned to her maid and said, "Speak of this to no one, for your life may be the price of endangering my son with false tales of woe."

"Yes my lady!" She bows and leaves quickly only to return with stew and bread for Prince Rewdan a few moments later.

Queen Jacqueline had led her second born son Rewdan into the tent and bid him sit upon a log by the fire. She smiled to herself as she saw that he could not help but notice the surprising child hidden upon her bed.

"I see I'm not the only one with a story to tell," he whispered to the wind.

His mother always heard, no matter how silent he may be, for she gathered her strength from the wind coming off the mountain. No piece of clean air was safe from her.

"That story shall be told to you by your brother Cirtap as it is his story to tell," replied the queen.

Her glee was easy to see. This pet had been good to her. Never had she had such desire to practice her craft since their father had died some four years past. To this day, not even mother knew why. Sometimes the sea merely carries men away.

"On to the story of Selrach, Mother." He had her full attention now. "We had docked at a village of the Plains People on Clear River. I accompanied Selrach to the Village House where we partook of wine with the local trader. Selrach was finally beginning to learn their language, so I left him early in the night to catch up on some sleep in the loft. I later learned that Selrach had stayed up very late into the night drinking and speaking of local gossip. One such legend had intrigued him in particular about a local girl said to be descendant of their sorceress queen. As absurd as it was, in his drunken state, he thought it had been our servant girl that had brought us our first drinks!"

After a hearty laugh he continued. "Selrach, being the foolish drunk, left in search of this meager girl by moonlight. Swearing it would bring him good fortune on his journey. Instead, he was never seen again. A raiding party hit the homestead of that very girl and left nothing standing. We searched for days before returning home yet found nothing more than the sheath of his sword."

He reached into his cloak and untied a spare sheath hanging at his side. His mother took it as a defiant tear slipped from her eye. "I swear mother, if I had any clue where to find the king of the Plains People, I would never have left without him. My only hope was that you would be able to see him with the clear sight of the wind."

"My son must be hidden from me. I have not seen him for nearly three phases of the moon." Now it was the Queen who whispered.

"Mother, where could he be that you, of all, could not see?" came Rewdan's faltering voice.

"Only within the Earth or the Sea..." her voice trailed off as they finally noticed Cirtap standing just within the door.

"We will find him again mother. I give you my word. For every man that hides him, two shall die!" Rage pulsed through Cirtap as sparks of fury dared leap from his soul. 'First the Raiders dare threaten my shore. Now word of them attacking my brother alone in the night. What cowards! They shall not remain unpunished.' He clenched his fists and started pacing just within the door.

"Calm yourself Cirtap, there is much yet to know. Come and tell of your victorious battle and my precious little pet."

"As you wish, mother." He too took a seat about the fire and shared a drink of water before he began.

"Two phases plus have passed since the day of mixed fortune. My scouts spotted a Raider's ship seeking the shore before a storm. We caught them off guard as the last longboat landed. Coming out of the woods, they were an easy slaughter. Unfortunately, two longboats carrying their leaders far along the beach were able to make water before my band of warriors reached them. However, I doubt they lived long at sea as the storm caught them approaching the open water. Only the sea king could help them there. I left their dead to feed the fish while Primo summoned me to inspect the cargo within their ship."

"You mean to tell me Primo actually 'summoned' you?" laughed Rewdan.

"Yes brother and with good cause, for I would not have believed it if not for my own eyes. Sitting upon a full harvest of wheat sat that girl. She was adorned in a fine linen gown laced down to her knees and yet untied. She had passed out after a very rough beating from the raiders.

Near death, they had left her bound and gagged with the cargo. Never have I seen such a sight. We brought her up river just as the waves began to crash on the shore. That night was as awful a storm as I have ever seen. Yet mystery upon mystery. Before the sun broke the horizon, the fury of the storm began to fade. I had just begun to sleep after tending her wounds when she woke. Black and blue from her beating and wearing more bandages than clothes, she rose to tend to herself. This half dead wretch of a child used the pot, combed her surprisingly bountiful hair and made some tea before returning to bed." Cirtap shook his head in disbelief. "Twice in less than one day I was actually shocked by that girl!"

"She sounds extraordinary indeed. Yet still she sleeps," mocked Rewdan.

"That is my doing," whispered the Queen. Now she had their attention. "I guessed the first day that she would not speak our tongue and do not desire for rumors to flow freely among our people. Instead I have been controlling her dreams, forcing her to remember. Now that you have returned, you can use the gift of tongue to awaken her memories and learn who her true protector is. Someone has been blocking her from me and I do not trust her to be set free until we know what power she holds and how it came to be that she rests upon our shore."

Cirtap put his hand on his mother's arm. "Mother, she wakes."

"Just in time," his mother said as she poured a fresh cup of tea. This time she added nothing but mint and honey to the water. She wanted the girl to wake as fresh and clear as if waking from a long winter slumber ready for spring. "Take this to her Rewdan and speak words of the Plains People. With luck she may know of your brother. Be gentle and slow in your persuasion."

She turned looking for her other son. "Cirtap, stay with her, as it was you who found her and freed her from bondage. She may recognize your face as one to be trusted, not feared."

"As you wish," was all Cirtap said as he moved to a log near her bed. When she rolled over and reached out a hand, he took it firmly in his and pulled her up to sit by his side. She leaned her head on his chest, as he offered her the warm tea.

Chapter Three
The Linguist Speaks

Their voices had been like music waking her from a dream. Eventually she began to blink in the light. Before all was clear, three shadows began to move. Strong hands held her firmly, lifting her into a world of waking dreams. Somewhere in the back of her mind she had been screaming in fear, yet she now found herself snugly wrapped in fur by a warm fire. The man from her dreams had changed. His hair was paler and he now sat smiling before her. A drink was put to her lips and down it went. Warm and sweet like the morning sun. A woman reached up and more light poured in where rain once fell, 'Is this also a dream?'

"Good morning young Miss," came a rugged voice beneath a short beard. He smiled as he sat beside her legs and took her hand in his.

"You may call 'My Lady,'" was her reply.

"Indeed, 'My Lady,' do you remember anything...?"

"Only dreams... Where am I?" she asked.

"You find yourself waking on the banks of the Muddy River in the land of the Cliff Dwellers. I will be your guide as you are my guest. You my call me Rewdan," he replied.

Her vision slowly became clearer as she was able to turn her head and see how much he looked like the man now holding her for the second time. This new man must have been somewhat older as he was taller and thinner in the face. He kept his beard trimmed short along his jaw while the whiskers above his lips were smooth. "Good Sir, a Lady ought not be so informal, I shall call you 'Sir' for a gentleman you are," she said.

"As you wish, My Lady," Rewdan turned to his mother and nodded.

She knew with that, all was going well. Her son Rewdan could be trusted to learn all that she could remember while Cirtap's arms made her feel safe. Trade goods needed to be tended to and it might look suspicious if the Queen lingered while Prince Rewdan related his latest stories of conquest to his little brother. So she slipped out of the tent as he turned back to the girl, knowing he would come to her later with a full translation of all that he had learned.

"You say you remember only dreams. Tell me of these dreams, perhaps I can help you to remember more." 'Let her rant,' was the key. He would soak up every word.

"In my dreams, I start out seeking strawberries. It is early and the day has not yet broken through the mist. Instead of finding fruit for my basket, I find a man. I know his face. I have served him once before."

Rewdan cuts in, "What do you mean by 'served.'"

"I recall looking up at him as he sits at a high table. He takes a drink and smiles as he touches my hand! Only the bravest of warriors, or the most foolish of men, ever dare touch me. So I put down the jug and left for the day."

Rewdan remembered that. 'The girl at the Village House, could it be her?' "What does he look like?"

"Like you... but not. He is much thicker about the shoulders and his hair is dirty and knotted by salty winds at sea."

Rewdan switches tongue as he looks at his brother, "She knows Selrach!"

"My Lady, where do you see him now?" Rewdan can't help but sound impatient.

"I am walking down the path along the coast when I see a massive foot reaching out of the bushes. Curiosity makes me break the bush away. He has been clubbed aside the head and begins to moan. When I lean over to look more closely at his wounds, he murmurs in a strange tongue. I ask him to speak again and he reaches up to me. His fingers slip around my neck as he grabs a hold of my head to whisper in my ear. 'Game afoot' is all he says. Then I feel cold metal placed in my hand. It is his long sword. I lay a kiss on his lips and lay my cloak over him before running back up the road. I never get to where I am going though. Something grabs me from behind and hides the light from my eyes. No matter how I kick or fight or scream, the light is kept from my eyes as I am pulled into the sea."

The men can feel her anxiety as she curls up in fear.

"My Lady, this man has been left far behind and long ago. You may no longer help him. Rest and eat. You must regain your strength," Rewdan said as he walked towards the door.

"Good Sir, you don't understand." She jumped up and was almost screaming without realizing she stood half-naked before two strange men. "He gave me his sword as I gave him my kiss. Do you not understand what that implies?"

"Indeed My Lady. You will take no other but he who you have granted a kiss. My brother, Prince Selrach of the Cliff Dwellers, now lays defenseless as he mistakenly gave you the protection of my mother's blood that was contained within his sword," Rewdan was angry now and clenched his fists as she stared at his eyes.

Shocked and at a loss for words, she could only say this as she sank back into bed. "He is not defenseless, my mother watches over us both as he now lies beneath my mother's cloak."

'Mother's cloak? What could that mean? Mother will know.' Rewdan switches tongue once moe as he looks out the door. "I must go fetch mother... and for decencies' sake, will you please get some clothes on her!"

"But what did she say?" Cirtap begged, confused by the outburst.

"Selrach gave her his sword before she was captured by the Raiders." With that, he had left his shocked brother looking at the girl who now lay silently crying on the bed.

'Without his sword he could be lost to us forever. Why would he give up his sword? Foolishly drunk indeed. Of all the brothers, he had to be first born. At this rate he will get himself killed before ever sitting upon the high throne,' he thought to himself.

Cirtap opened the tent flap and stepped into the light. Mother's camp maid had truly showed her worth today. At the sight of him, she rose with several trays laden with food. She had some foresight. Cirtap had not partaken of food before the morning hunt and now found himself famished. He held the tarp aside for her to enter. If she noticed the weeping girl, she said nothing of it. Cirtap grabbed the pile of clothes that had been forgotten at the head of the bed.

As he handed the maid the clothes he said, "My mother will need freshly washed bedding immediately and after that, I will seek your company, I have been lonesome of late. Make sure to have your daily chores covered. I do not wish for us to be disturbed."

It was code and she understood. A nod was all it took and she was gone. Later she would return with the girls clothes freshly cleaned by a hidden stream and would fit the girl into them. He would have water boiled by then. The guest would need to eat before bathing. Her hair would be combed and braided as befitted a woman of the Cliff Dwellers. Later, her dress would be covered by one of more local origin, giving her warmth for the coming snows and hiding some of her more dainty foreign features. By the end of the day she would be allowed to walk among the people as a mute from a distant inland village.

Rewdan found his mother walking along the cliffs beyond sight of the camp. He walked along her side and offered her his arm. They walked in silence while he contemplated his words.

"You were right mother," he finally said.

"How so?" she replied.

"She may have been the last to see my brother alive."

"Selrach has not yet passed, this much I know," came a scornful voice.

"Dead or not, he is lost to us and to you. Mother, she found him unconscious on a coastal road. He gave her his sword mother and she left him with nothing more than a cloak." They had stopped now as he stared out to Sea.

"Keep the faith my child, not all hope is lost. Let me tell you what I have come to know." She squatted down and took a fresh handful of earth. "My Son, you know that I learned long ago to gain strength from the wind in order to see."

He nodded.

"As a young girl, I studied at the Birthing Waters with the greatest seer of all. He alone braved the boiling mud for strength. However, I was not alone in my tutelage. Another girl and a young man also studied the forces of nature hoping to harness their own strength. We became friends and rivals in those short summers. We two girls were destined to become queens while the young man would sacrifice his youth to stay as guardian over the sacred water," she paused as if looking into the past. "My sister who studied the earth, followed the healing river out onto the plains to find a man in the high dessert, a man destined to be King. It is tradition of the Plains People to lead a humble life and so he still does to this day. He built her a home within the Earth where they first met and bonded. She then gave birth to two sons and one daughter."

"Mother, I have been to the plains many times. They speak of only two sons." She stared into him and he swallowed his words. "Unless you believe the words of a drunk!"

"Your brother was wise to drink water that night while the local drank wine. Secrets are not so easily hidden in a liquor filled brain." Again she grabbed another handful of earth. "My sister ran from the Raiders heavy with child some seventeen harvests ago. She birthed a sickly girl on a small farm and bled the last of her strength into the soil of the barren fields. Every year henceforth, that farm has grown even more bountiful crops. More than any other in all of the Plains. The gentle King was wise to leave her daughter there, for there she would grow protected by her mother's blood. Upon her fifteenth summer, King Kerill came to the farm and made a gift of her mother's cloak as was bade him in a dream. This is the cloak your brother still wears as he dreams of the girl screaming in the distance. Rewdan, you must understand, after he was jumped from behind, he too was beaten and left for dead. He chooses to wear the cloak now as a shield of life while he heals. The King has insisted that he reside within my sister's home throughout the harsh winter coming in order to regain full strength before avenging her daughter. My sister watches over my son as I must now watch over her daughter. Rewdan, it is time, we must go to the girl. She must send dreams of not only her safe arrival, but also of her health, to Selrach. The Kings Dreams of a harsh winter may be more foretelling than mine, thanks to his bride. We must break camp today and make haste for the Long House while she travels to with your brother. Come, there is much for your brother to learn of his coming trip and much that you will have to tell the girl."

Back at the great tent, the not so young girl almost felt normal again. Her head was clearing and questions began to whirl through her mind. 'When will the speaker return?' This other man (though most honorable and trustworthy as shown by his discretion), was a warrior who does not speak her tongue. Though the hours had passed with making herself presentable, she did not understand why so many clothes were necessary. She had regained much of her strength and was able to move about the tent, but daylight was quickly slipping away. She longed to see for herself what it meant to be among the Cliff Dwellers.

Finally he returned with an older woman. By the looks of her satin gown and fur cloak, possibly the Queen. The girl bowed and was waved to kneel by the fire while the three talked. She did not have to wait long until they gathered around the fire with her.

"Jannine," came the now familiar voice.

"Pardon?" She replied.

"Do you not remember your name?" Rewdan asked.

"As I told you before, all I remember are my dreams."

"Your mother was a dear friend of my mother, and as such you are named after her. This is my mother," he waved at the woman who graciously nodded back. "Queen Jacqueline, Sorceress of the Wind and ruler of the Cliff Dwellers." Now the girl looked scared again. "As your late mothers' spirit watches over my brother, so will my mother watch over you. So long as he is safe, so shall you be. However, my brother may be having dreams such as yours and with out the physical presence of your mother, he is now left in doubt. You alone can remedy this."

"How?"

"You must travel with my brother Cirtap to gather the healing water before the first blizzard locks it away for the winter." He looked at the other man who had brought her here and helped her to wake. Rewdan nodded at him as he got up and left. "Your journey will be harsh as winter comes early this far north and the mountains are very steep. I hope you can ride a horse as the approaching storms leave little time to travel otherwise." He reached for her hands and looked deeply into her eyes. "Jannine, this is very important, when you get to the healing pools you must first bath, than drink, then fill a barrel of water. You will find four pools as the river becomes a stream up the mountainside. When you reach the top you will find a man living in a simple hut next to a pool of boiling mud. Do not attempt to speak with him, but grant him the respect owed a King." He turned to the woman and took her embroidered handkerchief. "Lay this cloth from my mother at his feet, and then fill the smallest of barrels with mud. Once you have done all this, you must return with the water and the mud as quickly as the weather allows." He turned toward the queen, "Mother, I think that is everything."

"Make sure she understands all of my directions."

With a silent nod to his mother, he turned back to the girl, "Jannine, do you understand all that I have said?"

"Yes, I think. I must go to gather healing water before the onset of winter," she said.

"More than that, first you must bath, then you must drink, then you must fill one barrel of water. You must repeat this as you climb the mountain. Bathing, drinking and filling at each pool of water."

"Rewdan, make sure she knows to gather the water at the falls so that it is not tainted by her flesh," his mother whispered over his shoulder.

"Fill each barrel at the waterfall filling each pool after you have bathed. Is this clear?"

"Yes." She bit her lip and thought for a moment, "Rewdan? When shall we leave?" With that, they all looked up to see Cirtap entering the tent.

"Now," was all Rewdan said before guiding her out and into the failing light. The sun was setting behind the mountains as the camp was being packed onto wagons. A massive horse the color of rain clouds was brought before her, and Cirtap helped her to mount the steed by grabbing hold of her hips and lifting her body above his head. With the fear of her own life she took hold of the reins and saddle as if to never let go.

"I will see you at the Long House, Jannine. Safe journey to you!"

Rewdan gave the beast a slap on the rump and they were off.

Chapter Four
The River of Life

Cirtap led the way pulling three gray horses behind him, all loaded with barrels. Jannine's horse pulled another horse loaded with a tent, sleeping furs, and some basic camping supplies.

As day turned to night, Jannine could not help but think Rewdan had been kind when he told of the journey as the trail led them along a river that ran at the base of rocky cliffs. This trail was so rugged that it would surely become treacherous once the first snow began to fall, encouraging ice to form on the stones that made up the path. From time to time, Cirtap would dismount and help her down only to lead the horses along an earthen shelf skirting some rapids. It was good that she had slept so long and hard, for this trip was already wearing on her weak body. The horses continued on through the night, guided by Cirtap's instinct and the full moon. Cirtap must have known the path well for he never missed a step.

By daybreak, they had already traveled so far into the land of the Cliff Dwellers, that the river was now little more than a wide stream. Cirtap stopped in a clearing to let the horses rest while he took a nap. Jannine walked through the trees for a short spell before finding a warm sunny spot on the grass near him to sleep. When she woke, Cirtap had reloaded all the horses and was letting his water on a tree. He spoke to her, as if she could understand, then got a drink from what remained of the river. She followed in kind, finding a secluded bush behind which she found enough privacy to let her water run.

Next she filled a drinking bladder and approached Cirtap waiting by her horse. He bent a knee for her to hold on to his shoulders as he took a firm grip of her hips. Then up she went again and sat on the wooden saddle with both feet dangling down on his side of the horse.

Today Cirtap left the river, keeping the setting sun at his back. It was eerie as the sun spread their shadows through the trees. For Jannine, it was as if seeing trees for the first time, even though she did not yet know how truly rare these giant trees were, for their width was greater still than that of the massive gray horses they rode. The silence between the two was not so bad for it allowed the girl to fully take in the beauty that surrounded them. These great trees that seemed to touch the sky partially blocked a view of rugged mountains on their left while moss and ferns covered the forest floor. Eventually the boulders of the cliff face faded from her sight as they continued on a path straight into the heart of the forest that was growing darker with every step the horses took.

Cirtap continued on his chosen path as night began to fall. As any good Cliffman would, he had many skills of the forest. The small bundles of grass he had made while she slept were now being dropped into the ferns. They were too small for mere mortals to find but enough for the horses to smell. Even if it snowed, their hunger would guide them back to the glen. From the camp sight by the stream, the return trip would take a much different path up to the queen's village on the cliffs.

Eventually, Jannine could not help but notice how he no longer held the reigns. His horse, like all of them, seemed to now be on their own journey. 'Maybe they will lead us to the water when they get thirsty enough?' she wondered.

What neither of them could see, was the shadow of a woman slipping from tree to tree. She was gathering the grass and seeds not native to the dark forest while encouraging the horses on with the sweet smell of their green treat. She led them along the shortest path through the forest. She knew the most direct route to the plains and she knew why they had come.

As her daughter began to fall asleep, the essence of the late earthen queen stepped out from behind a tree, let her hood fall off her head, and whispered to the horse beside her, "Slow and steady now old friend, we do not want you to loose my most precious daughter, so near her destination."

Moonlight lit the grasslands as the horses finally broke free of the dark forest. Although mother had told him of stars to look for, it was not necessary. No fog yet lay upon the healing river, so he could clearly see the moon reflecting on the lake known as Deep Water, where the waters disappeared from sight to feed the wheat fields of the Plains beyond the High Dessert. They would easily be there by morning and collection could begin at sun rise.

Cirtap turned to tell Jannine (for what ever good it would do), only to see she had fallen asleep and was about to fall off her horse. 'That should have been expected. After nearly three phases of the moon in bed healing and half drugged by my mother, how could I expect her to stay awake much longer?'

Without the drowsy girl giving any notice, he took her reins and tied her horse into his ever-growing chain. Next he leaned over and gave her the mightiest of hugs, gently pulling her off her horse and onto his lap. Jannine took a deep breath and instantly felt her head dreaming of his strong heartbeat.

Somewhere off in the distance, another heartbeat grew stronger as well. Beat for beat, the dreams combined until three heartbeats rang as steady as a single beating drum.

Soon morning would come, and Selrach would awaken with new hope as the feeling of life had beaten its way back into his heart.

Morning did come to a small tent along side a mighty lake. After a breakfast of wheat rolls and boiled berries, Cirtap gestured for Jannine to join him by the lake. He pointed at the water then across to a small stream rolling into the lake over some rocks. He left her standing there staring at the water to pack the horses again. This time, he filled her saddle with a large fur. When he had finished securing the last of the lead lines, and was ready to continue the journey, he approached her with a smile on his face.

"Jannine," was all he said, then pointed at the water again.

'Could this lake really be the first pool?'

Cirtap was obviously not going to let her leave camp any other way. By the look of the growing grin on his face, it looked as if he was looking forward to this. With a deep breath, she took a first step into the water.

Cirtap laughed out loud and grabbed her arm, "You silly girl, you will drown if you try to cross wearing so much."

After rambling in some strange foreign tongue and making gestures that looked like drowning, he tried to pull off her fur cloak.

The harvest season was nearly at an end and the air was more than cold. If he insisted, she could get by in the shallows without her cloak. She let him have it and he flung it over her horse's flanks. Then he returned with his hand outstretched.

'What more could he want?'

Jannine took off the second dress given her by the maid and handed it to him. Again he flung it over the horses' flanks. Then again he returned. His smile now stretched from ear to ear showing all his teeth as he could no longer help but laugh.

This time he did not hold out his hand. Instead, he removed his own heavy cloak made of bear hide and hung it over the front of her chest.

The time for laughter had passed. As he tried to step behind her, she panicked and fell into the water. Cirtap immediately jumped into the freezing water after her and pulled her back up to the shore. As he began to rub warmth back into her shivering arms, he whispered, "Shh, it will be fine. My mother would not have sent you if she did not know you would survive. Come now, you must stay calm if you are to save your strength to get all the way across on your own."

Cirtap continued to hold her until she calmed down and remembered that he was the one who had untied her in the first place. As the sun climbed high enough to warm her face, Jannine resolved to get this done and over with. As if struck by lighting, the fear within her had been locked behind a heavy door and the once screaming voice of fear was now nothing more than a hollow echo. She pushed herself out of his arms and stood before him. With as resolute a face as ever he had seen, she shoved the cloak at him and began the daunting task of unlacing the cords that tightly bound the fabric of her dress to her body. After only a few moments, one side was loose enough and with a strategically timed breath, the fabric fell.

In such a short time, she had already begun to replace the flesh lost on the Raider's ship. Her skin no longer hung from her bones. In fact, Cirtap actually felt something begin to rise as he realized that the curves he now saw were not that of the youth he had originally assumed she was. Jannine stood there in the glorious sunlight only long enough to unbraid her hair. Her auburn locks fell just long enough to dance atop her buttocks as she shook it loose in the sun.

That breath of flesh was all Cirtap's hungry eyes saw, for she instantly dove into the frigid lake known as Deep Water.

The water here is truly deep and cold; far below the surface, Jannine let one hollow scream break her lips. She was right to be afraid and the fear instantly returned at full strength. Fortunately, her muscles remembered that which she did not. Her arms and legs instinctively began pulling with all their strength toward the light glimmering ahead. At the surface she saw that she had already made quite some distance into the lake.

When she turned to look around, Cirtap waved and mounted his horse. The race was on. He had to make camp on the other side of the lake before the water forced cold into her muscles.

The danger was as real as she had feared and he knew it. Cirtap could never have pushed her into such a cold body of water as this. In fact, if legend were true, the danger was twice what she now felt, for she would not be alone. Cirtap was not the only one watching Jannine struggle in the water. Only the purest of heart dared enter his dominion as vulnerable as she.

With only a glimpse of her thoughts, he decided he would let her pass. So pure and simple was she that all her heart and mind contained were memories of the first born son of the cliffs staring deep into her eyes out of such devotion... and one brief moment with his foolish younger brother.

Turning slowly, she could see some rocks not far ahead of where Cirtap was riding. He would beat her and have a fire waiting. Time was slipping away, but the water felt warmer now. Slowly she began to move across the water. Finding a rhythm, she pushed on ahead. The closer she got, the warmer the water seemed. So much so, that she was beginning to fear getting out. Finally she felt the sand beneath her again.

Cirtap was waiting on the shore with a bear fur... but something held her back. There was something she had to do. Deftly, she began rinsing her mouth with lake water as she turned around. Her body was so numb, Jannine could hardly think anymore. The rocks, the falling water... Something about the falling water. 'More than that, first you must bath, than you must drink, than you must fill one barrel of water,' the voice came to her as if in a dream.

As fast as she could, Jannine swam to the falls and drank till her mouth could hold no more. When she looked up, Cirtap had already grabbed the barrel and held it out to her. It filled quickly and she felt such relief to see Cirtap pound the lid into place. In one swift movement, he had her and the barrel out of the falls. He then left the barrel behind as he carried her immediately over to the fire.

Cirtap finished making camp around her without a single thought. Jannine's flesh was as pail as a corpse drained of blood and soaked by the rain, while her lips were as pale a shade of blue as the sky. Some relief came to Cirtap as he finally saw her begin to shiver. 'Half the men in my army could not have survived that swim,' he thought.

The lean-to was erected between her and the mountains. All the strength the sun could give her she would get. Tonight they would need to block the cold breath of the mountain. Mother, however, would find them easily enough. She had stained this tarp with her bloody hand long ago to grant protection to her children on their first voyage.

'Three days and the first barrel is done,' he thought.

He cooked himself a hearty stew from the dry goods he had brought while she slept beneath the fur. After eating, he decided to make an early night of it as she was still very cold and weak. He piled all the furs on top of her, then stripped himself and crawled under the furs to lay by her side. He almost let out a yell himself when he touched the flesh of her arm. For extreme cold seared from her body into him as he pulled her flesh closer to his. As he closed his eyes, he took a deep breath and clenched his teeth, waiting for time to bide by.

Once the first stars began to shine, Jannine began to regain consciousness and stirred, so he hushed her and pulled her body onto his chest. Again she heard his heart beating and her feet sought the warmth of his legs. Cirtap could hardly sleep that night, for as her body became warm once again, he began to appreciate why his brother saw her worthy of his sword. 'I could not have been more wrong when I saw her as a silly girl.'

Queen Jacqueline was also aware of this, and so much more, while watching them through the fire that night. She saw the way her son held Jannine. She looked into her dreams and memories of the day. So fresh and full were the thoughts racing through her young mind. As morning approached, the Queen also saw for herself how frustrated her son had been, all night long. He did not notice the full fire still aflame in the pit. He did not bother to wonder how it had lasted so long. He just searched the sky for the sun hopping the new day would not end like the last. Once he had found all his clothes, he began making a morning tea. The first log thrown into his fire broke the spell and mother could see no more.

Jannine heard the thump and asked, "How did the furs get so warm Cirtap?"

He turned at the sound of his name and came to sit by her side. After offering some morning tea, he handed her the pile of dresses and left for a walk.

The stream feeding the lake was shallow but wide. He followed it to a bend where he could see that it winded ever so gracefully up toward the mountains. Slowly he made his way back only to find the camp was no more. Jannine had taken little time making herself presentable for the day only donning her dress of the Plains People and a fur cloak. She knew she was up for another dip today and so had bundled the Cliffmaiden dress with the fur bedding. The tarp was quickly and easily stowed as were the cups and small pot. Jannine was walking up stream to fetch drowning water for the fire when Cirtap reached her.

This was awkward. He had only been so close to whores before. A woman's body was nothing new, but for him to be so close to one so pure as to survive the lake! Let us not forget she had already chosen his older brother. They said nothing when he could not help but take the pot of water from her before walking away to stir the hot coals.

'This will not do!' Jannine would not live like a helpless invalid being waited on by warriors. Granted she had been ill, but that time had passed. With a few twists of her wrist she had whirled her hair into a loop at the base of her neck. With that done, she set to mount her horse on her own today. She pulled her small train over to a large flat rock. She pulled up her skirt up so that the ties laced only down to her hip and in two steps, was ready to climb onto her mighty steed. Cirtap was just finishing with the fire as Jannine began riding up stream.

'When will she stop surprising me?' Cirtap had to get use to this. 'How did she get up there anyway?'

Such a mystery would have to wait; he was being left behind like a fool. He quickly mounted and started to catch up only to see a look of anger upon her face.

'What have I done now?' Like usual, he didn't understand women, and had made her angry. He took the lead only to be shouted at in a foreign tongue.

"Do you really think me so useless as to not even lead us up-stream?" she shouted.

Her words meant nothing to his Cliffman ears as he continued up the mountain.

"Ignore this you Cliff Dwelling Warrior!" With a snap of the line, she tossed him her spare horse and spurred her stallion on to a gallop.

She reached the next pool in little time. It was significantly warmer and smaller. Immediately she dismounted and disrobed. Before she had time to let her hair down, Jannine could hear Cirtap approaching with the other horses, so she dove in and quickly swam to the other side just in time for him to hand her a barrel after she filled her stomach with pure clean water.

'Maybe it is good for me to be angry.'

She smiled as the sun was not yet high in the sky and they were done with barrel number two. He secured the barrel and started up stream leaving her horse tied to a tree. Her dress and cloak were all she needed as the stream bed was growing sheltered from the wind by trees similar to that which they had ridden through only two days before. Getting back up will be more difficult this time, few rocks were as large near this pool.

Not far up stream she saw a tree with some low branches. After leading her horse over, she flung her cloak over his flanks and then climbed the tree. It was a little challenging to get her skirts up and a leg over, but it has awkwardly enough done. She then wrapped the cloak around herself and continued the ride up stream.

Jannine found Cirtap just around the next bend where he had been watching the entire time. With a simple nod, she took the lead and they rode in silence to the next pool. This time Cirtap turned his back while she changed. After she swam and drank she called out his name. Cirtap then walked backwards to hand her the barrel, and again, left her horse behind.

The trees are even taller here. Now how will she get back up? Her eyes searched the encircling forest while she dressed. Finally, she saw it. Not far from where Cirtap waited was a fallen log. 'I don't care if Cirtap sees how I got up, merely that I can get it done without him,' she thought as she took hold of her horses reigns.

Jannine walked her horse between the log and Cirtap. He held the horse steady while she hitched up her skirt and climbed the log. Balance kicked in when she stretched out a leg to the horse. Cirtap saw that she would surely fall, so he kicked his mount to sidestep and pushed her horse closer just in time for her butt to fall on the side of the saddle. It might have been funny if Jannine had not been standing on her newly healed ankle.

Cirtap had seen the ankle falter. He remembered why and respected her all the more for it. 'A warrior she might be after all. Such a wound will trouble her the rest of her days, yet she does not let it show!'

He knows well how that felt. His left shoulder still did not turn well after his most recent battle with the Raiders. As they came around the next bend, Cirtap remembered what his mother had said about the final pool and handed Jannine the packhorse. She took it back and followed as she had the day before.

The trail was becoming steeper. Trees blocked the view behind them and all that was left ahead was a mountain of rock. Trickling here and there was the clearest water ever seen as it meandered its way from the glacier to the river.

Cirtap dismounted and pulled the camp off her horse. When she leaned over to dismount, Cirtap reached a hand up as if to tell her to stay. Within moments, Cirtap had the lean-to erected and bedrolls out. He took her spare dress and hung it from the lean-to as his mother had directed. Then he unsaddled his horse and left all of the full barrels along side of the tent. One large and one small barrel remained with Jannine on a spare horse while the other three were tied to a tree to graze. Cirtap then unpacked one bag she did not recognize before taking the reins of the packhorse to lead her even further up a rocky trail.

Finally, Jannine could see the hut Rewdan had spoken of. It sat on a ridge some distance above them. No livestock could be seen. No outbuildings, no garden; the only sign of life was a thin line of smoke reaching toward the sky.

Cirtap knew no guardian would sit in the open. He had deliberately set up camp to tell all around that a girl had come to bathe. A girl who had already survived the first three pools.

By the time they reached the final pool, they both had spotted movement in the tree line below. They were being watched very closely. So closely that Jannine's skin began to crawl from all the eyes upon her. At the pool, Cirtap helped her to dismount and bade her to sit on the ledge. He put down the bag beside her and laid out a fur rug from his most recent hunt. Upon the rug, he opened the bag and laid out a comb with a glass vile of oil wrapped in the cloth given her by his mother. Then he took Jannine by the hand and bade her to join him.

'The easy part is over' thought Cirtap. 'Why do I have to be the one that Jannine trusts?'

After such a trip he did not think any man could do that which he must now do. He turned to stand on the ledge and struck his sword (containing his mother's blood) upright between two stones, for all to see. He then took the cloth given him by his mother and tied it about his head (rendering him blind). Next, he turned and knelt beside Jannine. One hand reached out and found her coiled hair while the other hand reached for a comb. Jannine, having no clue what was required of her, sat patiently and let her escort do what he must.

Cirtap combed her pail brown hair until it was as smooth as silk and reflected all the colors of the sun. He then proceeded to remove his vest, shirt, and leggings; causing Jannine to close her eyes. He then took her hand and helped her stand. By now fear was growing inside her again. As he let her cloak drop to the ground, she began to shake. Neither Cirtap nor Jannine knew whether it was more from the cold, or fear, but her trembling quickly became visible. So he held her close and hushed her to stillness. Jannine looked to his covered eyes as Cirtap tried to reassure her with a forced smile. She buried her face in his hairy chest as he began to loosen the ropes binding her dress. When he was ready, he lifted her face and kissed her forehead. She stepped back and the gown fell. He (wearing nothing more than woven short-pants), knelt before the fully nude girl and opened the bottle of oil. Beginning with her feet, he worked his way up slathering every part of her body being kissed by sunlight. Once this stage was complete he walked her to the ledge for all to see how she glimmered in the sun.

Several moments passed before she saw a man emerge from the tree line. He was very tall and slim wearing long pale brown robes. His yellow beard was as long as his hair that danced on the wind. He walked another winding path that lead to the opposite side of the pool.

"Why do you bring forth this young woman?" He asked in Cliff tongue when he finally stood level to Cirtap.

"I have been sent as her escort to ensure you that she is pure, and remains so, until the time comes that she should choose to bond," answered Cirtap.

"And how did you come to know her?"

"I rescued her from the belly of a raider's ship."

"I see. What all do you know of her?"

"Only that she is a Plainsmaiden born to the late Earthen Queen and that her memories were lost during her time in captivity."

"So be it written in the stars and so she remains. I approve this maid as worthy of the final step of purification and expect you shall guard her well until such time as enough of her memories are returned to her, that she shall make her choice with confidence in her heart."

The tall man then stood watch as Cirtap guided Jannine into the pool. She swam to the other side, drank of the falls and swam back to take the barrel from Cirtap. Once he heard the lid pounded into place, Cirtap held her dress above the spot she had entered.

While she swam back, Jannine could not help but notice how the stranger stared at her. As if filled with a father's pride, yet reserved! As if fear and concern overwhelmed his joy at seeing her in good health! Once she was again dressed in her thin gown of the Plains People, Cirtap redressed himself. He then removed the cloth from his eyes. Jannine took it from his hand and knelt before the stranger.

The guardian took the cloth from her without a word and examined it closely. After recognizing the mark of Queen Jacqueline, he looked up and said, "You would be Cirtap... Third born son to Queen Jacqueline, Apprentice of the Wind and Queen of the Cliff Dwellers?"

"My Mother proved worthy of the rank of Sorceress when my father first took her as his bride."

Manus looked at the girl, then at the young man, "As her personal Guardian, I entrust you with her care from this day on, until she chooses to bond with her chosen man."

"Yes Sir, I, Cirtap of the Cliffs, give you my word, that I will do all that I can for Jannine of the Plains."

The tall man then smiled down at her and waved her past with the small barrel in her arms.

She alone took the small barrel beyond and found the pool of boiling mud halfway up what was left of the mountainside. While Cirtap waited with the stranger, she quickly opened the barrel to find a wooden ladle. Scooping seemed to take forever, yet the deed was finally done. Pushing the ladle into the hot mud, she forced the lid closed yet again. Slipping back down the mountain took only a few moments, and she quickly found herself back on the fur. Cirtap bade her to hold the small barrel as he wrapped her cloak around her and slipped on her shoes. The horse was repacked, and he lifted his sword only when they were ready to leave.

As they began to descend the mountainside, a voice called down to them in the tongue of the Plains People. "Princess Jannine, daughter of the Sorceress of the Earth, you must remain as pure as you are today if you wish to be worthy of the man you have chosen, he that would be High King." When she turned to look, the stranger was gone.

Chapter Five
Snow on the Mountain

That night, and every night there after, Cirtap slept on the other side of the fire while Jannine slept beneath the lean-to, still holding the hot barrel of mud. It rode on the back of her horse, while the four barrels of water followed on the packhorses, now behind her. Cirtap kept the lead pulling the horse laden with their camp as they trudged along the mountainside.

Every day, when they stopped for the night, it was the same. Cirtap would make camp. He would then come to help her down and she would build a fire while he hunted for fresh meat; sometimes fish and sometimes rabbit. He was never gone long, but she was always waiting with tea by the time he got back. Every night while they slept, his mother kept watch through the fire and helped to push Jannine's dreams of the warm healing pool to her son, Selrach.

Occasionally, the Queen would slip into the dreams of her son, Cirtap. Time and time again she saw only one thing, the image of Jannine as she lay with him after filling the first barrel. She saw how her son held her so close, he could have taken her seal. She knew how her son felt as Jannine's body warmed to his hungry flesh. She did not blame him, with fresh meat every night and the warmth of the mud to keep her company while she slept, Jannine was growing strong once again, strong enough to be worthy of her son. Unfortunately she had already chosen Cirtap's older brother.

Jannine was also aware of how he felt, she could feel it in his heavy breath every time she walked by him. She noticed how slowly he let her down off the horse, pausing just shy of the ground to hold her close once again. She noticed how he gently caressed her legs when helping her to mount. Jannine had felt his eyes upon her lips in the morning as she drank her tea and every night as she nibbled fresh meat off a bone. Since the stranger had spoken to their backs from the healing pool, Cirtap had rarely looked into her eyes. There was often a sadness about him that could only be explained by the fact that he now desired that which she could not give.

Traveling with such heavily laden horses made the journey go much more slowly then either one of them had hoped. The horses had found the way back through the mighty forest to the original stream in no less then three days. From there, Cirtap had crossed the stream and followed a path into another forest. This new forest was much denser as many different trees fought for the light touching the slopes. They had stayed close to a ridge where the river dropped off below only cutting across to the mountain slopes when the land gave way to fertile valleys in the hillside. What had once been a mighty river, now looked like a distant stream. After several more days, the ocean could be seen from their extreme height on the mountain. Only then did Cirtap slowly start riding to the south-west, around the mountain.

Day after day she had seen the occasional village below, yet he never stopped or approached. The nights were just beginning to show the moon again when the snow began to fall. From a cliff, Cirtap saw the smoke of a mighty fire and pointed it out to Jannine. Beyond, the storm clouds rolling over the mountain, looked black as night. On this day, they road hard down the face of the mountain. As the snow began to blow, they approached a collection of buildings made of fallen trees. Now she understood why Rewdan had mentioned 'the Long House.'

It was long indeed. They all were. Several structures were laid out with short ends facing a circular gathering area. Many horses had been tied about and a great signal fire had been built on the rise above.

Mother knew how close they were and had prepared a feast to introduce the Out-land girl. Cirtap called ahead to some men who waved and ran to take the horses. A very tall young man, wearing a vest identical to Cirtap's, ran to help Jannine down. She smiled at him after recognizing his face as the one standing behind Cirtap when she first woke on the ship. He had to be a trustworthy man, so she gladly reached down to his shoulders and fell into his arms. Instead of placing her feet on the ground, he reached an arm under her legs and carried her to the entry of the largest structure. Rewdan was waiting to greet her at the entrance and gave her a massive hug, than kissed each cheek.

When she pulled away, his familiar voice said, "You must get use to our customs, oh simple girl of the wide flat Plains. Come see for yourself how affectionate we can be on a holiday."

Rewdan waved to Cirtap, who came over with a smile on his face. He had been waiting for this! Dearest brother would never mind a kiss of greeting. He heartily hugged the girl who had been his sole companion for two phases of the moon. He kissed her on either cheek then spoke to his brother while still holding his hand about the small of her back.

His brother nodded back and said, "Jannine, you would not deny a small reward to the warrior who safely guided you through the Dark Forest twice and returned you safely to my mothers house, would you?"

"Anything I have to give is his," said Jannine. She smiled at Cirtap who immediately tightened his grip about her waist as he pressed in on her lips.

'Oh how I have hungered for this,' he tilted his head and began to massage her lips with his, refusing to let her go.

In an attempt to breathe, she tilted her head back to open her mouth... only to have him lift her off the ground and slip his tongue into her mouth as gently as possible, while still forcing his way.

'Give it to me, please. Let me hold you just this once...,' he pleaded silently.

When she finally began to relent, he felt every part of her tongue with his until she began to feel him deep inside. A strange new sensation of warmth began to grow between her legs as her belly tingled like never before.

'Yes, feel within for me like I feel for you; remember my arms, respond to my hunger...'

Her mind was spinning by the time he let her go and placed her feet once again upon the wooden floor of the entrance. A crowd had gathered and began to cheer when Cirtap raised his arms as though victorious.

It took a moment for her to regain her wits. Then Rewdan noticed her lifting her skirts before swiftly kicking Cirtap behind the knee. He caught himself on a structural post and turned to stare at her in amazement as she slapped him so hard that her hand hurt and his face showed the rushing blood in his skin. Silence fell over the gathering as Rewdan caught her hand when she went to likewise strike him.

Such a sweet voice as hers sounded horrible as she spat venomous words at him, "How DARE you trick me."

Rewdan released her hand and bowed to her as he spoke in the tongue of the Plains People. "Forgive us Jannine, as my brother deserved all that he got. Then we can forget this misunderstanding."

"I don't know about, 'ALL,'" was her snapped reply. "Give me one good reason why I should forgive this outrage that will NEVER be forgotten."

"There was no other way for me to gain the gift of your tongue," came Cirtap's voice, only now he spoke in words of the Plains People. "As I am to be your guardian for the remainder of your stay, it is necessary for me to understand your needs."

"What magic is this?" Jannine asked as she stepped back in more fear than she could recall in her short memories.

"This is the Gift of Tongue, only granted to those who have traveled beyond our land and tasted the lips of a foreigner," replied Rewdan. "How else do you think I came to be so fluent."

"My brother is very popular among the whores," laughed Cirtap.

"And yet my face has been just as red more than just once, little brother," Rewdan loved to brag.

"Does this mean I can speak like the Cliff Dwellers now too?" Jannine begged when she finally remembered they were her friends.

"Far from it," said Rewdan…"You are too pure to take pleasurable gifts of another body."

'Pleasurable, that could be one way to put it,' the thought made her begin to loose strength in her knees.

The brothers noticed and smiled at each other. Rewdan spoke words of the Cliffs and sent most of the crowd away laughing while several men came to pat Cirtap on the back. Even though this runty girl dared strike the prince and Captain of the Guard, they still seemed happy to see her. Eventually the community had all retired for the evening to their separate houses. What remained of the feast lay inside the queen's Long House. So Rewdan and Cirtap both offered Jannine an arm and opened the doors wide for her to enter.

Jannine walked forward slowly as her eyes adjusted to the dim light within. Down the center of the great room lay one long open pit where the earth was covered in ash from recent fires. Wooden planks made the smooth floor that stood less than one of her feet above the earth. At the far end of the structure, she could see stones that continued the wall into the hillside. Four arches held four sets of wooden panels, each engraved with a different animal. Wooden platforms formed several elevations along the three main walls, allowing for many people to gather in warmth. The farthest platforms contained benches, and a woman who sat high enough to look down over the entire room.

Rewdan and Cirtap greeted their mother and explained the commotion outside. She looked as if ready to strike them down herself, and no doubt she would have had it not been for the red mark still upon the face of her youngest child. Jannine was seated on a bench below them and alongside the fire, while several older men still lingered sipping on drinks served them by voluptuous women.

One woman in particular was more than happy to see them. She also had long hair that lay low upon her back. All the hair that his girl restrained was that which would fall over her eyes. The rest fell free to fold upon her shoulder or dance across her bountiful breasts. She seemed more than flirtatious and even dared to scold Cirtap when she caught him watching Jannine. He then said something that pleased her and she left smiling. Jannine thought it odd he would be so tolerant. She was obviously a servant, and with breasts as bountiful as hers, she had to be a nursing mother to some child.

The evening grew late and Jannine was becoming sleepy from all the meat and roots brewing in her stomach. The plump woman returned as a signal for the older men to retire. She stood silently in the shadow by the entrance as the Elders approached Jannine. Rewdan gestured her to stand as each man in turn grasped her by the shoulders and gently lay a kiss upon either cheek. When the last one shut the door behind him, the plump young woman approached.

"Jannine," said Cirtap. "This is my jealous bed mate. Her name is Blossom."

"What do you mean by bed mate?"

"She is not well enough born to become queen, yet she still gives me a son and warms my bed when I am not traveling with the guard. She is enough of a pleasure to have around that my mother tolerates my pet and allows me to feed my hunger when stuck at home."

"You mean you have known her flesh without being bonded?"

"I cannot bond with her as her station forbids it. We rescued her also from the Raiders. Only she had been their captive from childhood and was already un-pure. She has remained a servant in our house for now two summers past." He bade her to sit beside him and he held her as closely as he had Jannine only a short time before. "She will be your guide around the village this winter. I hope you can become friends. If you like, I may assign her to you permanently. Tomorrow, you must follow her, as she will introduce you to each member of the village. You are expected to try every task along the way in order to learn what your body remembers doing. Just like swimming Jannine, there will be some things that your hands will know even when your mind does not."

"Come Jannine," called Rewdan. "Mother bids you rest upon the bed you have chosen." He led her up a series of platforms beyond the Queen's high bench. With a small lamp in his hand, he points at a panel in the wall with a inlaid carving of a mighty black bear, "Go ahead and give it a push."

With a little grunt, it falls back and slides to one side.

"This house was built especially for our family by my late father," Rewdan says as he leans into the stone cavity and places the lamp inside a small niche. "Each of us have our own sleeping chamber for winter months, mother's is to the right while mine and Cirtap's are to your left. As my brother Selrach is first born, you will sleep closest to my mother. A small covered pot should be in the far corner if you should need it."

"Are you not done with her yet dear brother?" Cirtap laughed as he climbed up with his eager pet.

"Near enough young stud. Don't make up for too many nights all at once will you? I want to get some sleep tonight."

"How could I, our guest's gift still haunts my lips."

Jannine blushed and Blossom smiled as he opened his own bedchamber door near the far wall.

"Are you two enjoying yourselves?" asked Jannine.

"Actually, very much so, yes," said Rewdan. "Rarely have we been able to say a word with out mother knowing. Now we can say anything with her sitting next to us and she is forced to remain ignorant. You have no idea how glorious your gift is."

"Will you please stop calling it a gift," Jannine begged as she sat in the door.

Rewdan knelt before her and looked into her eyes as she started to cry, "But it is, only a woman who enjoys being stirred can release her tongue. If there is no pleasure, there is no magic." He laid his hands upon her knees and looked longingly into her eyes. "That is how I know you are still damp between the thighs. I would give anything to have been lying on that road. The thought of what awaits my older brother within you makes me angry it had to be him. For no other man could I hold back from such an experience. I do not envy my younger brother having to purify you. He will have a hard time ever seeing another woman's face upon the body laying in his bed." He said as he got up and opened the door beside her. "Sweet dreams sister, I expect you will enjoy my brothers bed!"

That night she had trouble getting to sleep. Her body ached as if needing to be held, and every time she closed her eyes, she saw the hungry eyes of her Cliffman. Images of the stolen kiss haunted her mind, and every time she tried to think of Selrach's face, she felt Cirtap's hands about her waist. When she could handle no more, she rose and left the small chamber. Below, in the main hall, the coals still glowed enough for her eyes to adjust to the room. She assumed everyone else was sleeping, as the room was perfectly silent. So she walked out to the entry and was bitten by the cold. There she saw that the snow had already fallen deep enough to show footprints. Two had left and one had returned. Suddenly, a cloak was laid upon her shoulders as she felt hot, hungry breath on her neck and ear.

"Can't sleep either," said Cirtap.

"Why?"

"The kiss I stole will allow me to pleasure Blossom no more." He stepped back and blew warm breath into his hands. "I never would have believed fetching water could change a man so. Blossom will have no part of me for quite some time now. She left with the same look on her face that you had before swimming in the Pool of Deep Water."

"You really are in trouble then."

"Truly..."

"How am I supposed to sleep now?" she asked as she leaned back on the timber and stared at the moon.

"Pardon..."

"My body will not relax and my mind will not stop turning."

"What do you think of?" Cirtap asked.

"The differences between you and your brother."

"Me and Rewdan are very different indeed."

"Not Rewdan."

Cirtap faltered. The stolen kiss had far more repercussions that he could have imagined. "Let your mind not dally on such things, a thief has no right to what you have saved for Selrach."

"I'm only just beginning to feel what that might be."

"You cannot be feeling anything," denied Cirtap. "You are still pure of body."

"Then why is Rewdan right? Why does he know that my belly is releasing a warmth that still dampens my thighs? How could he know about that which has never happened before!"

"It must have happened before, at least once, or you could not be so fluid now."

"What are you talking about?" she was snapping again. Fatigue and frustration had worn on her patience.

"The first day when my brother Selrach laid his hand upon yours, a part of you must have wanted more. That's why you remembered him, that's why you gave him your cloak, and that is why you were forced to grant him your first kiss. The Elders of the Plains People know it takes time for a woman's body to warm within. That is why a man with hopes is allowed to take the woman of his choice walking. When she is ready she will begin to dream of him and yearn to feel his arms about her by moonlight."

"This makes sense, only, my problem being that I do not know whose hands I ache for, all I remember are his eyes. His big, dark, hungry eyes... They feel as if he has seen me a hundred times and still wishes to see more. I can not breathe with out seeing those hungry eyes."

Cirtap put his hands around her and held her close. 'There is more to a man then just his eyes.' As he leaned down to kiss her again, she buried her head in his chest and began to cry. 'Why can't you be mine?' He let her step away as a stab of pain shot through his heart. Cirtap left her standing there and returned to his bed where he lay staring at his lamp until morning dawned.

Chapter Six
Remembered Skills

Jannine did not emerge until the morning meal was almost done. She said not a single word as she nibbled on dried berries and nuts. All the while thinking of the words she had felt in the back of her mind during Cirtap's touch.

Eventually, Blossom brought her a drink, then pulled on her hand. It was time to make the morning rounds. They left the Long House and walked from step to step about the Village Gathering. First Jannine tried basket weaving and made a horrible mess of it. Next she tried sewing. Shortly there after, she was allowed to work the flour for baking. By midday it was reported that she possessed no womanly skills other that preparing and serving meals. By late in the day, Rewdan had spoken with Cirtap. They agreed to let her try some of the men's sports, thinking it would be funny at the bare minimum.

"Jannine," they called in harmony, "we have some sport for your weary hands."

"Sport you say," she new they were up to something, but couldn't resist. "I suppose I could use a good laugh, too." She had them with that!

The trio walked together in silence toward a clearing below the village. Jannine could see the ocean from here and waves could be heard crashing on a rocky shore far below. Near the middle of the field, several trees had been left standing stripped of bark and cut to a height no more than a full-grown man.

"Let me see how well you ride," called Rewdan. "I will even let you pick the horse."

Just within the tree line on the north side of the field was a roped off area where several horses stood grazing. Some were saddled and a couple bore nothing more then ropes about the head. She ducked under the rope and walked straight passed all the saddled stallions to a little brown mare.

She led the mare to the men and said, "I think she will do."

The men just shook their heads; she had gotten the shortest, oldest horse in the whole herd.

"If you insist," said Rewdan. "Now it is our turn."

She hopped up and easily swung a leg over the short little pony while both men chose very large muscular silver stallions, easily more than twice the size of her mare.

"Now Jannine," Rewdan said upon their return, "We have to catch you! If you're little filly can out run us, you win."

"Any boundaries?"

"None".

"Jannine, anywhere that little horse will take you, you can go. To make this even more worth your while," Cirtap said, "I will give you that horse if you are still upon it come sunset!"

"Brother you can't do that, mother would take your blood for granting such valuable property to a woman not your own."

"Until our brother returns, we should treat her with the respect owed a woman of our own. Besides, a mare that small is not such a valuable thing."

"Too true and well called brother." They turned to look only just in time to see Jannine waving from the cliff. She kicked her mare and with a good yell they were gone. "Shall we get to the chase then?"

"Indeed, for there is game afoot."

Jannine rode hard along the cliff until she heard the pounding of horse's feet behind her. At the last moment she jerked on the reins and squeezed with her thighs. The mare turned sharply, cutting off Cirtap's stallion and sending him hurling toward the ground. His hand had been ready to grab hold of her cloak but it was now pounding the earth instead. Rewdan merely laughed as Cirtap yelled, "She is getting away!"

Jannine continued to ride hard weaving between the trees and found that the mare was working its way back to the glen. Rewdan caught a glimpse of her and spurred his horse on. Cirtap saw him change direction through the trees and doubled back along the cliff. By the time he reached the clearing, the mare was just emerging from the forest. He charged at her, passing Rewdan as she turned and sprinted up the hill.

Her horse had much less weight to carry and did not slip on the pine needles as theirs did. She regained her ground and spun the horse around. 'Now where should I go?' She turned and took the other path down towards the cliff. This one wound down hill much more than the other had.

Eventually she came to a clearing where men were practicing archery. She grabbed a rope out of the hand of a man standing near her and tied it to an arrow. She then shot it into a tree some twenty paces away. The remainder of the rope was then tied to a tree on the opposite side of the trail. Time was up. Hoof beats were pounding down the trail. She kicked her horse with all her might as the men dropped their bows and jumped out of the way. No sooner than she was halfway through the clearing than did she hear first Rewdan, than Cirtap yelp and hit the ground as their horses came to a screeching halt.

There was no time to look, they would be after her again soon. The panting horse was not use to this and slowed to a trot as they wove through the trees until she found a secluded stream. Only then did Jannine let the horse drink while she tried to think of what to do next.

From the flat of the ground, Rewdan spoke to his brother in the Tongue of the Plains People so that his Warriors would not understand their words, "Brother, I love you and am as loyal to you as any other, but I give up."

"There is no shame in that, but how are we to tell her."

"I don't know, I don't care. My back hurts so bad! I fear I may cry before your men."

"Now there might be shame in that, only if I do not beat you to it. How are we going to explain this to mother?"

"Brother I would give you this stallion if you could answer that."

"My lord," spoke Primo, "If I may be of assistance. I too took the Gift of Tongue while still a youth trading in the Plains."

"Really?" asked Cirtap.

"Oh yes, I remember now, a ripe and eager maiden near the Clear River, as I do recall," said Rewdan. "I hear she passed the following harvest attempting to bring forth a child."

"That would explain why I never received word of her coming. Nevertheless, I could fetch the princess for you." He looked around and said, "All those present are loyal to you above all. You could swear them to silence my lord."

"Indeed, Primo, you have just reminded me why you are first mate, and thusly I grant you my brother's horse. Take it and fetch the girl; with our most sincere congratulations, the mare is hers."

"Yes My Lord, and thank you my Lords."

"Now you have given away two fine horses that will require explanations to our mother," Rewdan said as some men came over to pull them up. "Let me not forget to mention an explanation of our most recent injuries..."

Down by the creek, light was dimming. Jannine wanted to keep the horse but was worried she might be lost for the night if she did not turn back soon.

"My Lady? My Lady, where are you?" came a distant voice in the forest.

"Who speaks the Tongue of the Plains People?" she hollered back.

"Primo is my given name, First Man to Prince Cirtap, My Captain. He bids me send you his congratulations in a fine victory."

"But, the sun has not yet set," she yelled.

The same man that had carried her to the entry emerged from the trees not far up the creek; she braced herself to run thinking it might be a trick as he began to speak. "The light does shine brightly upon my lords, however, they wince as it shines too brightly into their eyes."

"How could that be?"

"My Lady, I left them still flat upon their backs, still winded from the fall."

She looked up suddenly realizing how badly they were hurt and yelled, "Flat on their backs! STILL? You must lead me to them immediately."

"This way my lady."

Her horse was finally willing to move again, so they wove through the trees quickly. It was a different path, but they caught the men on the road just outside the village.

"There be the wicked woman who would hurt us so. Look brother and see how sorry she seams," cried Rewdan.

Cirtap smiled, never had he seen his brother suffer so. "Don't suppose you can repair what you have done? It would save me a lot of words with our mother."

"Let me see your back," she said.

The brothers looked at each other, both hurting too much to volunteer.

"Little brother, you asked," said Rewdan.

"I did at that," so stop he did in the middle of the path.

Jannine slid off her horse and walked around to his back, "Well?"

"Well what?"

"It is your turn to disrobe."

Rewdan shook his head and smiled, "You heard the woman, off with it already."

"You are going to enjoy this... aren't you brother?"

"Right now it is all I have, little one."

"I'll show you 'little' as soon as I can stand straight again."

Off came the cloak, his vest, and shirt. For the first time, Jannine truly saw how badly he had been scarred by previous battles. Deep cuts had left his entire torso scarred with unorganized lines. Some longer and wider than her longest finger. As she had guessed, two lumps near the middle of his back had stepped out of line with the others.

"I need you to lay down," she said.

"I don't think we can do that here, you are supposed to be for my brother and there are too many witness of your purity."

"We all know you wish, but I wasn't asking," she informed the man as she took his cloak and lay it folded on a flat piece of ground. All the men gathered round to see as Cirtap reminded them that they were all sworn to silence. Jannine bade him lay down, then pushed him over on his belly.

"I want your back, not you! Primo, I need your help. Come and take my hand. It will be your job to make sure that I do not fall." She dropped her own cloak and slipped off her leather shoes. "Cirtap, so long as my feet are on your back, you must not move your hands from your sides."

"Your what?"

Too late, he could no longer breathe as she had already mounted and had proceeded to wiggle her toes along his bones. Pop after pop could be heard as her heel moved from one joint to the next. Cirtap cried out in pain a couple times causing some of his men to reach for their swords. Primo, however, waved them back, and so they waited. Finally she dropped and sat upon his rump. Using the full weight of her body, her hands slowly pushed the pain out of every muscle. Cirtap felt sleep approaching by the time she slapped him on the shoulder.

"Up with you now, my hands barely have enough strength left for you brother."

"You have got to be joking," said Rewdan.

After standing up tall and straight, Cirtap yawned and reached for the sky then bent backwards as the sun would upon setting to bed. "Big bro, if you are so foolish as to not even give her a try, I'll hug the earth again. This woman can put her hands upon my flesh as much as her little heart desires." These words were spoken in the Tongue of the Cliff Dwellers for all his men to know that no further harm would come.

With that, many of his men knew it would be a while, and so set off up the trail returning to the village for the evening meal while the Plainsmaiden healed Prince Rewdan.

Nothing more needed to be said to Rewdan however. He had

this cloak and shirt off as fast as his back would let him.

"I think I will take my new horse to bed now my lord," said Primo.

"As you will, I have the ladies hand," said Cirtap. He nodded to Primo, who mounted and rode off through the woods.

Shortly thereafter, Jannine had done all she could for Rewdan and he also stood and stretched as his brother had.

Then turned on her and said, "I feel good enough to pick you up." Without a moment to protest, he did just that and Jannine found herself flying in circles high above his head. When he finally stopped, he lowered her down just enough to hold her in his arms and lay a kiss on either cheek. "Promise me you will do that every night and I promise to sleep alone happy," he said.

"Anything to be of service my Lord. Well, almost anything."

They all laughed when she said that, so Rewdan placed her sitting sideways on her horse that the trio might begin to walk back up the path.

"How long do you think it will be before I can make Selrach sleep happily?" she asked.

"I believe you already do," said Rewdan.

"When will I be able to lay my hands upon the flesh of his back?"

"Not for several full moons. The water is already not passable as the first snow made the shallows cool enough to welcome the great monsters of the deep," answered Cirtap.

"Could he not travel by land?"

"By horseback it would take nearly three phases of the moon and only a fool would travel the plains when blizzards are expected to be so abundant."

"This is Selrach we are talking about. He is no fool. He would ride hard every day if the King would grant him horses and a map," snapped Rewdan.

"You don't really think he would, do you?" said Cirtap.

"If he is fully healed before the first snowflakes find the plains, he wouldn't hesitate. You know how he treasured that sword, and I have never seen him seek out any other woman. If he has any inkling where to find them, he will ride," Rewdan knew his brother too well to think otherwise.

"Than I shall pray for him every night. I will pray that he comes for me and not the sword," whispered Jannine.

"Why not the sword?" asked Cirtap. "He will avenge you with it."

"No he will Not! It has already been tainted by a Raiders hand. He will have a new sword. One of such craftsmanship as to be worthy of the High King."

With these words, the brothers looked at each other and thought back to their childhood. Only their Mother and the Guardian new of the legend foretelling of a King to rule over all four lands. A single look at each other and they had already decided to speak with their mother about this tonight.

"Jannine, I want you to call to him," said Rewdan. "Call to him in your dreams..."

Chapter Seven
The Tea That Gives Wings

The evening meal was waiting for them in their mother's Long House, it passed silently as the men waited to have their mother alone. As the crowd finally began to disperse, Rewdan whispered to his mother. "I think it is time for you to make tea." She looked at him curiously... "Jannine will need wings to help her dream."

"And what errand shall we send her on?" asked the Queen.

"She must deliver a message to my brother..."

"May I know what the message is?"

"The Bride of the High King sleeps in your mother's Long House."

"The High King?"

"Jannine says Selrach deserves a new sword crafted of the finest metal, 'worthy of the High King,'" said Cirtap.

"Ask her how she comes to know this..."

"Jannine," it was Rewdan who called to her. "Come and sit by the high bench, my mother wishes a word."

She rose and sat upon the step at the queen's feet, "What can I tell the Queen today?"

"My mother wishes to know how it came to pass that you now refer to my brother as the 'High King.'"

"When Cirtap and I left the warm pool with the barrel of hot mud, the guardian said to me that I must remain as pure as I was at that moment if I wished to be worthy of the man I chose, 'he who would be High King.' That is Selrach, is it not?"

Cirtap now inwardly shook at the thought of what he wanted as recently as the night before.

Rewdan translated word for word what she had said to his mother, who never wavered. When he was done, she spoke to him in return, then rose and began making tea.

"My mother bids you sleep well, she also bids you happily dream of her eldest son. Tonight you shall sleep not only in his bed, but also in his clothes. His shirt and cloak already hang within his door. Take this tea to bed with you. It will work fast, so drink every last drop quickly as soon as you are dressed and ready. We will all stay up and take turns praying for you while you sleep. Jannine, when you find my brother, tell him 'ride home hard and fast.' Make sure he remembers your kiss and also make sure he knows where you are waiting"

Fear was beginning to creep into her again, 'What could be in this tea?' She took the drink from the Queen and crawled inside the bedchamber. Everything was waiting for her just as Rewdan had said. Jannine changed, drank, and then lay down, waiting for sleep to take her away.

"Tonight is what I have been waiting for, for now twenty five years past. The sword she spoke of is already being crafted. The horses were sent directly to the mines on the night you arrived. The mud contains the strongest fragments of metal available to mortals. The pure water will be used to cool the metal in such a way that the craftsman will be able to forge a sword lighter, stronger and greater than any sword currently in existence. Now, we must hope that your brother can get here before the raiders learn of our plan."

These were the words heard by Rewdan and Cirtap over the fire that night, after which not a single word was spoken. The whole night through, Jannine slept and dreamt while they watched through the flames.

The wind carried her soul on the clouds that night, over the forest, around the mountain, across the Muddy River and south of the Deep Pool. Far beyond the wild prairie, she found a small farm. Such a small place would not easily be found if not for the stars. One well fed the house and barn, while one skinny little road lead to a village. Here she stayed and here she called.

"Selrach, speak with me... Selrach, speak with me..." A sleepy man stepped out of a hole in the ground and looked around. He wore a pail cotton shirt and buckskin leggings under a tattered old wool cloak. He had been sitting by the fire when he suddenly felt an overwhelming urge to take a walk. The breeze whispered through his hair a silent lullaby until he walked over to lie at the foot of a mighty oak tree.

"Remember me... remember me... remember..." His lips became as warm as they had been every night since waking in the fog along the shore. His heartbeat steadied and his breath deepened. As he reached up, he heard her words. "Come to me Selrach, come to me... your bride awaits your hand..."

He sat up now as wide-awake as ever and found himself yelling at the air, "Where are you? Where are you Jannine?"

Fog collected about his feet and began to form a thin column before him. "I sleep upon your bed, within your Mother's Long House above your mighty Cliffs." The breeze blew and the smallest essence of a hand reached out to him... "Ride Hard, Ride Fast. Ride hard, Ride fast. Ride hard, ride fast...." The voice was gone as the sun broke the horizon.

Garth, first born son of the Late Earthen Queen, came up to see what all the yelling was about, only to find his guest reaching into the air. "What has happened Selrach?"

"She risks traveling by clouds to call to me."

"Who?"

"Your sister."

"That cannot be, she has not the gift!"

"No, but my mother does! I must ride immediately. Please offer my gratitude to your father for I must take a horse."

"Not without me your not, besides you are as yet still unarmed."

"My mother would not send a call to me if my sword was not waiting."

"You know as well as I that that is impossible."

"Perhaps. Yet I know my mother, She is always prepared and must know by now how well I fare. Besides, do you see that little cloud yonder? See how it travels all alone. She is showing me the path. I must start now while her trail still leaves light upon the sky."

"I can see that you are confident in this gift, we will ride and take four of my best horses. FATHER, awaken! Today we ride!"

The two men clasped hands and set to the barn.

Jannine did not rise until late in the day. Her last thought was of the trail of dust left in their wake. Soon she would meet her brother for the first time and her man would stand by her side.

Chapter Eight
Blossom

The last of breakfast was waiting for Jannine beside mother's bench. The family had stayed up all night watching, waiting, and listening. Fatigue wore on them as she rose afresh. The glimmer of hope that radiated from her face told them the last thing they needed to know. He was on his way.

Jannine ate meagerly that morning as her nerves began to wear on her stomach. Last night, she had seen him clearly for the first time. By the glow of the early morning sun, she had seen for herself what a mighty man he truly was. Where she was little more that a scrawny girl just turning seventeen, he was a hardened man of twenty-four. Yet as thick of the arms as Cirtap, he had the long legs, gentle hands and hungry eyes of Rewdan. Could she truly be worthy of such a man? He had traveled the mighty sea and traded with more than she knew. This was a man of the world that had fought for the sake of his own life on countless occasions, while she could not even remember her name!

More than that, Jannine had had a taste of his hunger last night. She still felt him pulling on her and wondered how she could ever please him. 'How will it be possible for me to ever satisfy his needs?' (That which she knew nothing of.) Yet here of all places there was no one to guide her, to teach her, to grant her the instruction she now desired. 'How long will it take him to ride if they continue cutting strait threw the desert?'

The snow had been gentle but steady. Even below the mighty trees, the piles no longer drifted. Within another day, it would easily stand above her knee. "Cirtap," she called.

The weary man smiled as he sat down beside her, "Yes, my future Queen?"

'Why did he have to say such a thing?' she thought as she took a deep breath to find the words. "My mind is racing from my dreams of the night. Do you think it safe for me to ride? I wish to make my mind as quiet as the breeze."

"My Lady," came Rewdans' voice. "So long as you are among the Cliff Dwellers, you shall always be safe."

"You took the words out of my mouth brother," said Cirtap. "However we should send someone with you. Blossom, perhaps?"

"I think that would be best." Jannine was grateful for the suggestion knowing full well that a ride with that woman would be silent indeed. Rewdan sent a young man to fetch Blossom and the horses. When Jannine had finally made her excuses known to the queen, she grabbed her fur cloak, only to find her horse, and Blossom atop Cirtap's steed, waiting just off the entry.

The ride out could not have gone quickly enough. Her body was already becoming ill from all the anxiety she hid within her soul. So many thoughts crowded into her mind that she now felt that she would truly become physically ill. Finally she reached the cliff. Standing alone with the wind in her face, she finally felt peace. So she just stood there and closed her eyes, breathing deeply of the salty air.

This was the moment Blossom had been waiting for. She looked and saw how the tide rose high enough for the sea to no longer foam. Grasping her opportunity, she grabbed the virgin and jumped with her into the sea below.

Jannine opened her eyes as a scream burst from her lips. The ground was rushing past her as if falling in a dream, only this was no dream. The harshness of this reality hit her with the frigid water of the sea. Blossom was prepared and pulled both cloaks free, then held Jannine tightly about the neck while floating on her back into the cliff.

Jannine gasped for air as she saw earth and rocks suspended above her head. 'Where is Blossom taking me? Why is Blossom taking me? This water hurts as much as that of Deep Water only there is no life to be gotten here...'

Cirtap, in his ever vigilance, had sent two of his most trusted guard to watch over the women. From some distance within the trees, they had seen Blossom grab the one destined for their Lord Selrach. In shocking disbelief, they watched them fall as if suspend in time. Her blood curdling scream would echo through their minds for all eternity. For as hard as they rode, their horses reached the cliff only in time to see the bottom of their dresses, with feet floating behind, disappear under the cliff. Without a word to each other, they turned, each grabbing the reins of a horse, and rode as hard as they could back through the snow to tell the royal family.

Cirtap was enraged at the news; Rewdan had just left for a hunt, so he called for Primo. His mother only had time to grab him by the arm as he ran out the door.

"Do not challenge him my son. He carries your brother's sword now."

She let him go at that.

They all knew about the caves. The Raiders had been sent off many a time before. How foolish he had been to not have it checked after the battle. Worse yet, his own pet had betrayed him. He would make sure that she did not live through the day. Not even their son could save her from his wrath.

Primo followed the prince in silence, knowing his moods too well to do otherwise. All he had time to hear was that the princess had fallen into the sea. How or why he knew not, but he would serve his captain in anyway he could. They rode down to the stream and then the river. Riding hard the entire way, they reached the sea when the tide had just begun to release the first strip of sand. Together, they hugged the cliff and doubled back. In little time they could see the largest cave at the base of the cliffs.

"We will leave the horses here," Cirtap said dismounting. He stood for a moment looking down the beach then said, "Primo, you must swear to me before we go another step, that even at the cost of my life, you will see Jannine safely returned to the house of my mother."

"As you wish my Lord," he understood fully as he himself had shed the blood of the sea once before upon this very shore.

"One more thing,"

"Yes my Lord"

"The treacherous whore who once shared my bed, shall not see the sun rise."

"Yes my Lord."

Her bare feet on the stone allowed her a new cense of her surroundings. More than a dozen men, all in poor health, hungry, cold, and bitter for their environment... stood in the shadows against the wall staring at the entrance of the cave.

One young man had stepped forward, smiling, as he pulled a cloth from his belt to bind her eyes before holding her on his lap near a fire beep within the cave and around a bend, far from the sight on the beach; yet still able to overhear the clear echoes of his Lord's old pet's interrogation.

"But sir, they say she is a princess!"

"The Plains had no daughter!"

"No, the queen died giving birth to a bastard!"

"You will hold your tongue! Never have I heard such outrageous accusations! Why, the late queen was as humble and loyal as they grow in the Plains. How dare you dishonor her memory!" He screamed as he slapped the girl with such force that she fell back on the stone floor of the cave.

Jannine felt her pain and flinched, raising her bare feet off the ground as she rocked back into the Raider's arms.

"Shh," the young man whispered in the tongue of the Islands, hoping to sooth her. "You must stay calm if the fire is to grant you any warmth."

"What?"

"Shhh, rest my little bilingual one. We will have you home soon enough. Trust me. I let you down once before, now that I have you back, I will do all that I can to make amends. Oh my pure little Plainsmaiden, I am so sorry we had to leave you behind." he said as he gave her a gentle squeeze. "Oh how I have worried about you."

His voice was quickly drowned by the echoes of the Seafairing raiders.

"My King, the Prince approaches with his first man"

"Now we shall see how much truth lie's within my old pet. Bring them out when I call. Captain, I do not wish for our guests to return with a count of our numbers."

"I understand."

He positioned himself in the darkest shadow on the far side of the opening and silently waited for them to approach. When they were just within ear shot, he let two arrows fly. The accuracy in his shot was clear to all when they both landed squarely between the feet of each man stopping them dead in their tracks.

The first man shouted into the shadows, not in the tongue of the Sea, but that of the islands. "Oh Captain of the Sea, today we come in peace. My Lord has lost two women that he wishes to retrieve."

'He came for me!' she thought as she sat up and leaned forward, hoping to extend her sight by reaching a foot to touch the boulder they sat behind.

"I am told that one is not his to retrieve."

At these words, Cirtap almost reached for his sword. 'No, I can not show my true desires; this must be a peaceful negotiation of sorts.' "Tell him they are both mine and I shall prove it if he likes."

With out a word of doubt, Primo raised his voice and relayed his Lords words to those hidden in the shadows beyond.

A few moments later, Captain Merrick stepped forward to the edge of the shadows looking like the rat that he was, soon followed by two young women. Both soaking wet, with their hands bound behind their backs and both wearing blindfolds. "Tell the prince that he may have the One... familiar with his touch."

'It worked, now if only Jannine could understand my ruse.' After allowing time for the translation, he handed his sword to Primo as a gesture of good faith. Then he walked slowly toward the two women. Even soaked they stood apart from each other. While Jannine stood like a sapling tree shivering in the wind, Blossom stood her ground firmly. The extra fat produced by the next child already growing within, had insulated her well for such conditions.

Prince Cirtap drew his short blade and held it in his hand while he ran his finger tips across the cheek of Blossom. 'Dirty little back-stabbing whore,' he thought as he tipped the blade into her flesh. She turned her head in fear and stepped back showing a line of blood. Blood left behind for all to see.

He then turned to Jannine and ran the blade along the pail flesh of her arm. 'Please know my touch. Feel my warmth and know I come to help.' She was so cold that she only felt the pressure of his hand as his words melted into the back of her mind. When she did not flinch, the blade left nothing more than a scratch. He then stepped behind her and placed his hand in hers. With a flick of his wrist, once again, the blade sliced through that which bound her.

As further proof before all the men, he intended to give them a show to remember. He left her standing where she was, and walked slowly back around to the front of her, allowing his hand to trail on whatever he desired. 'Oh to know such flesh that I would save for my brother. Oh Sorceress of the Earth, grant me one more taste of this flesh. Let her hunger for me now like I have silently hungered for her.'

He then re-sheathed the small blade. With the confidence he had seen in his brother Rewdan (a world-renowned lover), he wrapped his right arm around her waist and his left arm around her neck. As he leaned her back so that she lay within his arms, he whispered in her ear, "You must now think of me as my brother, my future Queen."

He laid his lips upon hers as she rolled her head to meet him and slowly opened her mouth to his. The deeper his tongue penetrated her mouth, the wider her jaw fell open until their tongues were dancing and her face could no longer be seen beneath his hair. She reached up with one hand so that both her free hands locked behind his neck as she pulled herself up to his chest. When he slipped his right hand lower, she arched her back and moaned. Her leg instinctively began to curl up to him, so he slipped his hand even lower and took a firm hold of her thigh, then lifted her up to his chest as he stood. When he finally took a breath and kissed the side of her mouth, he lifted her again so that both legs lay across his arm.

She kissed his beard and laid her head on his shoulder. As he began to walk away, she prayed, 'Oh mother, please let Selrach be as gentle and warm as this.'

Many of the men still within the cave could not help but croon at the sight. This made Cirtap smile as he carried her out of the shadows. He did not say another word to the Captain of the Sea. There was nothing more to be said. He took his young piece of flesh home that day, without ever drawing his sword.

"Let them go," ordered the Sea King, "and load her in the boat. We ride the coming tide home today. At least the child she carries may make a decent offering to the sea."

Cirtap was right. Blossom would not see the next sun rise.

They rode hard all the way back to the village and made it in record time. Lookouts on top of the cliff reported to the queen what little they could see. That being that Cirtap carried a freezing cold and dripping wet Jannine onto the shore.

Back at the Long House, water was being boiled and stones heated. Sleep again she would, in order to heal yet again. Cirtap was still carrying her when they came through the door.

She looked like a bundle of fur as he laid her upon the floor, and none dared stay when he instinctively began undressing her. The clothes had kept the cold on her body, and another moment might be the difference between life and death. Only the Queen was permitted to help as he did not stop fretting until Jannine lay within the warm water and opened her eyes.

"This is the second time you have pulled me from the cold," she said.

He smiled and took hold of her hand. "We have to stop doing this," he said in her native tongue. "People will begin to talk."

"Let them, it will only tell your brother of the depth of your loyalty."

'She can see no evil at all,' he thought. "Help her to rest mother, my brother deserves a woman of strength on the night of their bonding." His mother believed the sincerity in his voice and only nodded. "I'm off to organize a signal fire. If the next storm reaches us before Selrach, he will need our guidance."

For only twenty-one summers, his mind had learned the art of words well. For the first time, he had actually fooled his mother. A fire he would make ready, by the next day, he would have half his men working on cutting timber on the high bluff. For now, he needed to be alone.

Primo saw his master walking into the forest as the first stars began to shine. Only the fatigue from last night would force him to sleep. Primo had known Cirtap since they were both no more than sixteen summers and in their first battle. He had sought to hide behind a tree when Cirtap found him and put a blade to his throat. He had instantly dropped his sword and begged to die quickly swearing he would never fight the enemy of his enemy. After learning that the Sea King had taken the boy from his mother, Cirtap spared him and asked him to seek revenge by serving his enemy's enemy. Primo swore a blood oath that day and has been grateful ever since.

He alone knew how the kiss would haunt his Captain. He alone could be trusted to guard that secret well. So later that night, he took a horse to his Captain. Following his prints in the deep snow was an easy task, even for the Islander. Cirtap knew he needed rest and climbed on the horse while still allowing silent tears to fall. Fortunately, all were soundly shut away by the time he returned, allowing him peace to wash the salt from his face.

Chapter Nine
Greetings...

When morning came, Cirtap carried Jannine from his brother's bedchamber to a rug by the fire. She lay there sipping hot tea and broth until late in the day. The men worked through the midday meal and returned to a feast as the last of the sun shone. It heartened the spirits of all the men to see how Jannine had risen once again. She smiled and her cheeks were flushed as she walked from man to man serving all the beer they could drink. Rewdan, Cirtap and Primo all took turns translating tales told her by the men and all laughed late into the night. Only upon the Queen's request did the gathering disperse and every man there had to kiss Jannine goodnight on this day for word had spread that she would bring their future King home.

That night Jannine dreamt of the wind blowing through dry grass. She dreamt of a fire between two men. She dreamt of four horses tied to a tree by a trickling stream flowing down to the Muddy River and then blew a whisper to them... "Rest well for tomorrow you will ride harder than ever before."

Two more days came and went. A surprisingly warm wind blew

out of the south that melted much of the snow. Even the Muddy River was running high enough for the herds to gather one last time. Once the signal fire had been built, the men left for the last hunt before the snow locked them in for the winter. When they returned late on the sixth day, after her calling dream, Cirtap and Rewdan found Jannine pacing within the Long House.

"What could have you distressed at such a glorious time as this?" pushed Rewdan.

"He comes and I am not ready."

"He could not come for several days yet. Besides, what have you to be ready for?"

The sudden look of fear in her eyes should have answered his question, but he was in no mood to be observant.

"I am... not worthy of him."

"I'll not hear such nonsense," shouted Cirtap. "Never before has our world seen such a worthy bride."

She fell to her knees and wept into her hands as Primo knelt by her side and listened.

"How can I never please such a mighty man," she whispered.

Primo said nothing but offered her a cloth to wipe her nose. Then he went to the men and spoke softly in words of the Cliff Dwellers. A few moments later, Rewdan came to her side.

"Jannine, trust me when I tell you this, my brother is a wise, gentle, and patient man. I will speak with him and you will see; there is nothing to fear within these walls, least of all my brother. If you have any doubt still lingering in your mind, know this, Cirtap has tasted that which will please our brother. You have left such a mark upon his lips alone that he cannot sleep for his dreams of you. Something lies locked within you that pleases even me, and I've seen how even the guards can not help but lay their eyes upon you. I grant you this, should anything happen to my brother, many a quarrel would be fought among those who would seek you as their bride. Including Cirtap and myself. So do not fret on that which you do not know. The knowledge you seek will come only when your need calls for it."

She took comfort in these words and laid her head upon his chest while she wiped the last of her tears away.

Jannine still could not help but pace for the rest of the day. If not for what happened on her last ride, she would gallop the nerves right out of her. Instead, safety called for her to remain within the shelter of the village.

As the day wore on, everyone had something to do but her. The hunt had been very successful leaving countless furs and pounds of meat all needing to be cleaned and made ready for storage. The next storm could not stay off long and with the moist warm breath off the sea to feed on; it would be all the stronger. By late in the day, all were weary; so the Queen ordered that the most basic feast be prepared. Her servants had been cooking the first of the meat for half the day. When the meal was finally cooked, every member of the community was made welcome in her hall as they had worked very hard and deserved an early rest. The rest they could finish tomorrow.

Shortly thereafter, a scout came down from his perch by the signal fire; two men had crossed the river riding four horses at full gallop. He had run into the hall to warn the guard and accidentally sent a panic running through the people. With so many clustered in one building, it would easily make a deadly trap, and soon, everybody scrambled to get outside and scatter before the strangers could arrive.

Prince Selrach and Prince Garth arrived shortly thereafter to a very confused gathering, just as the last sunlight faded behind the trees. Half out of breath and sweating from the hard ride, not a sole recognized him except a slender wisp of a young woman standing on his mother's entry. Every one quieted when she spoke and the royal family emerged to translate.

"Greetings... oh weary travelers from the Plains. Please forgive the confusion. Although you have been eagerly awaited, none but I expected you to arrive so early as today."

"Greetings are not all I shall take of you tonight," came the outrageous reply. Some men approached the hooded man with swords drawn after Selrach spoke these words.

Then Cirtap pushed his way through the crowd, sword in hand, and stood before the still mounted man. He struck his sword into the ground and yelled, "No man but my brother dare cross me to take a single thing from the purest of brides."

Still wearing the cloak and hood, Selrach dismounted, stood face to face with his brother and hugged him. "See what loyalty I return to. Never could I have dreamed of such a welcoming. It is heartening to know how well my people would fight for me."

He removed the hood and all but the royal family bowed. He then flung the tattered old wool cloak upon his horse and walked passed his brother toward his bride. As he wrapped an arm about her, he called out to his people in the tongue of the Cliff Dwellers. "I take this woman from you now with many thanks. For I know you have cared for her well. Tonight I take her to my bedchamber, not as a mere woman, but as my bride. If it pleases the Elders, she will even provide proof of her worthiness for all to see. When next you see her again, she will be my bride who carries my blood, and that of my family living and yet to come. Now, for all to see, I kiss her, as my bride." He then turned to look her in the eyes and whispered words of the Plains People. "Jannine, my sweet, woman of my dreams. Grant me once more a kiss from your heart."

She looked up into his eyes and reached to push his soiled hair from his face. This was the face she knew from her dream. Those were the eyes she sought to find in the dark. So she stood on her toes, as he pulled her to him, then closed her eyes and allowed their souls to combine. Not a single person cheered, for this was the kind of kiss best shared in the solitude of the trees. Had they been on the plains, she would have granted this to him while they walked. Yet here for all to see, they stood alone.

When he felt he had had enough to satisfy the time, he quietly escorted her within his mother's house. Primo saw to the horses, even recruiting a couple other men for they would need a thorough rub down after such a hard ride. Garth however, was made welcome by the rest of the family as his sister granted her hand to the Cliffman. While they enjoyed a quiet bite to eat, Garth remained unable to properly greet his sister through out the entire evening, for Selrach occupied her ears, eyes, mind, and heart.

Finally, Garth rose and addressed the family, "For a man who has not laid eyes upon his own flesh for almost two years, it pleases me greatly to pass on the blessing of the Plains People upon this union. No doubt lies within my heart that my sister is made welcome by the finest of families. May all her sacrifices make her worthy of you Selrach, and may our mothers always watch over your children," he then bowed and left the building. He would sleep in Primo's small house during his stay. From him, he could learn all that had come to pass in his sisters' new, if not short, life.

Jannine however, took that as a cue, and walked the circle granting a kiss on the cheek of each member of the family before walking alone up to the bedchamber.

The men all watched as she shut the door before speaking in words of the Cliff Dwellers. "You must not let her wait long tonight," said Rewdan.

"Why?"

"We found her crying in this very room when we returned from our hunt this morning," came Cirtaps' reply.

"Whatever for?"

"Selrach, she has no memories, no mother to speak with, and her total experience with men consists of a kiss your dear brother here stole seeking her tongue," Rewdan said, conveniently leaving out the fact that it had been his idea.

"I had already guessed that much dear brother," he said with a laugh and a slap upon Cirtaps' back.

"You don't understand how pure she is Selrach," said Cirtap.

"How so?"

Rewdan and Cirtap looked at each other, and then Cirtap shook his head. It was left to Rewdan... "She fears that which you have to give her. She may even be terrified of how much pain may be involved in the giving of her first blood. She is even more afraid that you are too large a man for her to... satisfy."

"The poor ignorant girl has convinced herself that all she has gone through is in vain. That she will be unable to please you and thus prove that she is unworthy of being your bride," spat Cirtap.

This was a harsh reality Selrach was unprepared for, "What can I do?"

"Be gentle Selrach, wait for her to welcome you."

"But I promised an offering… what if she cannot provide?"

"Trust in her inner strength my son, and the stars will grant what you need," said his mother.

With that, enough had been spoken on the matter. Mother, Rewdan and Cirtap went to bed leaving him standing before his door.

Chapter Ten
Bonding

As she crawled into the stone chamber, her hands reached to the wall to help her keep her balance as she fought to straighten her dress and close the door behind her.

'What I would give to know my mother on this night,' she thought as she knelt in the dark and began removing the heavy Cliffmaiden overdress. Once the cloth was lifted over her head, a small flame burned within the corner niche. 'Who lit the flame?' Jannine thought in a panic. 'The door is still closed!'

'Jannine... my precious little one, do you not wish for your mother's council?' came a woman's voice from the back of her mind.

'Mother? Is that really you? They said you were dead!'

'My flesh does rot, but my essence lives on within the earth.'

'Oh Mother.'

'Daughter of the Earth, tell me... What gives you cause to call on me on this night?'

'Selrach will come for me soon. I do not know what to do. I do not know what will happen. I am so worried... so scared...'

'Jannine, know this. You have my gift of thought. Use it and follow your heart. Selrach is a good man and you are as strong as the earth. Trust in these facts and no matter what happens, you will be all the stronger for it.'

'But can I trust him?' she thought as the anticipation began to feed her fears.

'Trust in the flame. So long as you are within the earth, I will not allow anyone to harm my child.'

Though few, the words of his brothers had been direct. He now stood contemplating his next move and actually found a piece of fear. When he opened the door, he found her sitting in the far corner holding her knees. Still wearing the tightly bound dress of the plains that she had worn the first time he had laid eyes on her. Even her hair remained coiled on the back of her head. By the light of the flickering lamp he saw her crying for the first time. He would not have believed it, if not for his brother's words of warning. All evening she sat by his side holding his hand. She had never stopped staring into his eyes. Even when he asked for a kiss, still soiled from the journey, she had not hesitated. Yet as he closed the door behind him, she still did not move.

The massive man crawled over to where she sat and thought hard on what his first words should be, "My dearest sweet Jannine, do you know that I have dreamt of you every night? Not a soul dared mention the possibility of harm coming to you in my presence the entire time I lay weak from the attack on the road. Your brother and father recognized your cloak still clutched in my hands when a friend of yours brought me to their home in a wagon. For six days and seven nights they fed me and bathed me while I lay hot with fever. Never did your cloak leave my side. When I finally woke, I had dreamt of my brother's face before you and knew that you were safe. Then and only then, did I rise and take of food within your mother's home. A sculpture of her stood in the center of the great room and I marveled at how closely your face resembled hers." He lifted her face and caught her eyes. "Every day, the first and last thought to touch my mind was that of your kiss. You granted me the full gift of tongue that allowed me to not only live, but to return to you so quickly." More tears began to fall. "Jannine, tell me, do you really think yourself unworthy of me?"

She nodded.

"Do you not understand that I dreamt of you every night? I lay with you, and our hearts beat as one while your cold body recovered on the shores of Deep Water. I laid my hand upon your head as you slept every night. These gifts were all granted to me by you. So pure is your heart that your mind has always been open to me."

"But it was not your hands upon me."

"My brother did as our mother bade him. No more and no less. Though I count every moment till you will trust me so with your flesh." He put his hand down and touched her bare foot. "I know that our time in the sun has been far too short. I can only hope that the hours we have spent within each others dreams mean as much to you as they do to me." She bit her lip and stared once more into his eyes. "Come and lay by my side. I wish for you to feel my heartbeat in the flesh," he said as he took her by the hand and pulled her toward the empty end of the small chamber.

Just as she had always dreamed, his heartbeat was strong and steady. Jannine could barely make out the pulsing of his neck by the flickering light. She closed her eyes as she breathed deeply of his masculine scent even stronger for the journey. After a while he laid his hand upon her thigh. 'Oh Jannine, please trust me.' When she did not push him away, he pulled her hips closer to him.

He could feel her breathing become shallow upon his chest! If not for the silence and the small space, he never would have noticed such a little sign. But since he had, he moved so that his eyes could lock with hers. 'What can I say to make her less afraid?' "My dearest sweet Jannine, as my bride, I have something for you. But I promise, if you can find it within you to let me hold you so close as a man holds his bride, I swear on our unborn children that I will not give you more than you can take."

She still did not move, but when he took her hand in his to kiss it, she squeezed his fingers tightly. He kissed her again and this time she held her breath and pushed back. He then let go of her hands, wrapped his arms around her, and then kiss her again he did.

After allowing her several breaths, he sat up and lifted his shirt over his head revealing his muscular torso. His hair was paler and softer than Cirtap's and his arms, though just as large, showed fewer scars acquired in battle. As he turned to lay back down, he noticed how her eyes fixed upon his flesh.

"This flesh now belongs to you," he said as he pulled her up to sit before him. As she took her hand to lay it upon his chest he said, "Come here and know me as I wish to know you."

Her dainty little fingers caressed his curly hair then spread over his shoulder. When she had worked her way up to his neck, he tilted his jaw ever so slightly. His beard was short and not yet full. It still had the softness of youth about it. His ears hid under tangles of hair unevenly cut above the shoulder. She pushed aside a tendril of hair that had fallen into his eyes.

"It will hurt badly enough to make me bleed, wont it?"

He had to be honest, "Yes, you will bleed. Though I hope you will not feel the pain."

She dropped her hand and looked confused, "How can it come to pass that I will not feel the pain?"

He smiled and pulled her close. So close that he lifted her skirt and placed her legs upon his. When he finally had her as close as he wanted her. He blew a hot whisper into her ear, "Some women have been known to enjoy what their man has to give them."

He put his legs together lifting her to his thigh so that he could kiss her again and again eventually leaving her mouth and slowly moving down her neck. It was no feat for a man of his strength to lift her, and so he gently laid her down upon the fur, still kissing ever lower until stopped by her dress. He then worked his way up while his hands worked their way down. 'Oh how I want to know what you have been hiding,' he thought. Ever so slowly, he caressed her thigh. Up and down slid his right hand. With each stroke, he unbound another row of cordage binding her dress to her. When he had worked enough free, he lifted her to his lap again. Her eyes were closed now and her head tilted dizzily. He could feel himself becoming impatient, and so took deep steadying breaths.

The rhythm of his heart was felt through her hands still clutched about his neck. She felt his breath and breathed deeply with him. 'Oh how I want you,' came a foreign echo in her mind. He buried his lips into her neck and felt her jaw flinch. Only then did he let her pull away only to see the first mark the night would leave upon her body. "Did I hurt you?" 'What an impatient idiot!'

"Just a pinch."

But her eyes were now alert again and her voice was as strong as ever.

'Such a little pinch was all it took to bring her back.' This night would be longer than he thought. With out a moment's hesitation he had to take advantage of what little progress he had made. Staring deeply into her eyes he removed the top half of her dress and lay her down. Her arms instinctively covered her chest and her legs locked together but it was no matter now. The rest of the gown was easily slid down and off her feet. This he did slowly hoping to stay her trust.

Before lying down beside her, he deftly untied the cord near the front of his waist allowing that part of him that would grow more room to breathe. He then took a long deep breath as his hands caressed the length of her body. 'For a humble maiden from a farm, your flesh is unbelievably smooth.' The thought struck a nerve in his mind and he took hold of her hands, pulling her up to him. Her locked knees instinctively sent her feet behind her (as he had expected) so that they knelt before each other.

He sat back and enjoyed the sight of her for a moment. Truly rare it was indeed for a woman to have such smooth even skin. She naturally had no hair upon her arms, legs or belly. His hands told him how smooth her back also was. The thin tendrils, that only he would know, confirmed that she was more than of age. Yet without a single scar and such slender hips...

He sat in awe. "Do you know how rare you are?" he asked.

"What do you mean?"

"The sight of you can only be described as being the first to wake and find freshly fallen snow."

'Is that good?' she thought.

"An entire body so fresh, so clean, so pure...   And all for me!"

For the first time, he sounded as nervous as she felt! "Why does your voice fail you so? You, destined to be High King?"

"You have not yet heard the full legend, have you?"

She shook her head.

"Legend tells that he who should take the purest of brides shall be granted power over the Sea by those who control the Earth and Sky. Only by controlling the three most powerful elements can I gain the knowledge and power that will secure me as High King. You, so pure and strong, shall be my keeper. She who would yield the elements at my command."

"But I have no such power!"

"You don't, but our mothers do. When my mother passes, they will join to watch over us and heed your prayers. Your heart will guide our world, just as it gives me pause on this night."

"How do I give you pause?"

She looked scared again.

"Jannine, if I were not so concerned about you sharing pleasure on our first night, I would have taken you ten times by now. I can't help but want you. The more I try to be patient for you, the more my body aches. My brothers were so concerned about your inexperience, now I am not sure if I can do what I must."

Now she had a hard time keeping his eyes.

She leaned over and kissed him sweetly and took his hands. This time, she got up and pulled him up to his knees as well. "Oh my Selrach, I do not fear **you**, I never could. I only fear that which I do not know. I ask you now, not as your virgin bride but as an eager young woman." She looked up and into his eyes. "Could you find it within you to guide me? Then I will learn to please you."

He shook his head in disbelief at these words, "You do not understand, you have already pleased me."

"I understand enough to know that you still have something to give me." she leaned in and he put his arms around her.

"There is no need for that now; we still have much of the night," he kissed her again and they fell in each other's arms. 'Oh woman, if only you knew how grateful I was to finally have a worthy bride. If only you knew how long I have waited.'

He knew her limitations to him were few, and so he again began to ravage the rest of her body. 'Oh how I will prove my gratitude...' he thought as he kissed her chest and looked up to see her close her eyes.

Very quickly, he felt her begin to rise.

For the first time, Jannine was responding as he had hoped she would. Her legs began to shudder after his touch. Her breath jumped when he licked and kissed that which he desired most.

'Oh woman, never have I tasted a virgin's seal. To think you saved it for me!'

He lowered himself upon her thigh and felt the tension in her muscles, even her back began to arch as if asking.

'For such lean muscles, you are so strong...'

Now her kisses bit of hunger as her innocence was already fading away. When his knee pressed between her thighs and found little resistance, he put his hand below the small of her back and felt her lifting herself with a moan. He then wrapped his other hand behind her shoulders and lifted her up before lying down upon her with her legs wrapped about his waist and her arms about his neck.

His hunger was so great now that she could hardly stand the fury of his breath upon her chest. 'Oh take it, please take it...'

She reached up and pulled him to her for another hungry kiss and felt him pushing. Not just upon her lips, but also between her thighs. She wanted his mouth and sought it out, his tongue made her shudder and rise as he pushed with all his might. He pushed so hard that her head rolled back and she gasped under his first penetration. He kissed her neck as he slowly pulled back, allowing her to fall. Then she looked into the dark shadows of his eyes and lifted her head to kiss him again.

'Oh, mine, all mine...'

Moments later he pushed again, and her hands dug into his back as she fought to control the pain. 'Oh woman. Please take it all, Oh please, I wish you could take it all...' Another moment and she was pulling with her calves. Tears streamed from her eyes as she kissed him anew. He said not a word, but pushed so long as she pulled. 'Oh, yes... thank you, thank you my bride.'

His back was as raw as that between her legs before he was through. They lay there together while she caressed the hair on his chest. When he rolled over dripping with sweat and unable to breathe any harder, she laid her head on his chest and listened to the pounding of his heart.

"You look tired..." came a soft voice.

"You are an amazing woman," he said while caressing her back.

"How so?"

"Few women have been able to receive all I have to give. To think it was only our first time..."

"I only wish to please you."

"Oh... a memory such as this night will give a lifetime of pleasing memories."

She smiled and laid her head back on his chest. After a moment of watching the thumping in his throat, she felt the urge to kiss him again. It was time for her to show how much she had learned. She lay herself upon his body and tried to leave a mark within his beard.

'No, no, no...' He took a deep breath and pushed her up by the shoulders. "You have already done all that is required of you tonight. Please, I could not hold back so long again after tasting the bounty you have to offer. Let us sleep and you can heal. Next time it might not hurt so much."

"You wished that I would enjoy, and your wish was granted. If the next time will hurt less, then I am ready to take it now. Please allow me to show you what I've learned."

She did not wait for his answer and instead began kissing him. She followed the trail of hair below his belly and found the gift he had kept hidden.

'So she likes my little friend already!'

She watched it grow in her hand and understood how it could have hidden so long. Her fingertips caressed every fold as the skin revealed itself to be as smooth as she was, and felt herself becoming ready again. She released his muscle and hooked her fingers under the top of his leggings. She then gave a defining pull, and caught him off guard.

As he sat up and stared at his leggings, now around his ankles she heard him think, 'What on earth is she doing?'

She couldn't help but smile while pulling slowly and gently, until they were off and in the corner.

'Now my daughter, if you wish to bond with this man in Plainsmaiden fashion, you must allow him full sight of your true beauty...'

Jannine sat there for a moment listening to the guidance offered by the flame and let him watch as she finally released the mass of hair bound at the back of her neck. "You have given something to me. Now all of this belongs to you."

He watched it fall like water in the moonlight and could not help but catch his breath. The pail brown hair remembered the curls within bondage as she shook out the massive waves until they fell like silk around her body. She then crawled toward him, like a cat in the tall grass, slowly allowing him to enjoy the light dancing on every curve of her body as it was slowly revealed by her falling hair. When she got to where he sat leaning on the far wall, she rose to meet his lips with hers.

'Oh woman, how you torment me...' Selrach thought as he slipped his hands under her perky little breasts.

When she had her fill of his lips, she raised yet even higher on her knees and pulled his head down to her chest. With both hands, he took what he wanted, 'Oh sweetness, grow for me...' he prayed.

He licked the tips of her nipples until her knees could no longer hold her. When he let go, she clung to his shoulders for balance while trying to breathe. 'So they will grow...' After several deep breaths, she looked into his eyes and gently kissed his lips one more time. When she leaned forward with her whole body, he predicted her next move and laid his hand on her hip.

"You don't have to take my seed again."

"I hear your words as clearly now as the first time you uttered them," she whispered as she lifted her leg and slowly dropped herself upon his fully rigid muscle. Her exhale came like a whimpering moan as he pushed down on her hips and bit into her neck, causing her back to arch yet again.

For as much as she wanted, she could not take this much for long. He knew this, and when she fell, he rolled with her. Still so deeply connected, he pulled her by the hips back into the middle of the fur. Jannine could hardly breathe now as he pushed her open with the weight of his entire body. Her breath came and went with his weight. Her fingers dug into his back and refused to let go. Her blood mixed with both their juices making her much fluid than before.

'Oh, you are so smooth,' he thought finally feeling free to push and pull to his own quickening rhythm.

The friction met with the ache inside her belly and he heard her voice gasping in his ear. "Please Selrach... I need it... please... give it... to me... please...!"

Her claws moved lower on his back and her legs became painfully tight on his hips, so he sat up just long enough to take her hands in his. He then pushed her arms over her head and held them there with the weight of his entire body while he gave her all she had asked for. Forcing her to scream out as her back strained to pull the arms free that he held firm.

She would feel him shudder within several times before he would finally fall to her side. Jannine was only then allowed to curl into a ball. As every muscle in her body began to shudder from the exquisite joy of bonding, he rolled onto his side; pulled her even more closely into the curve of his body, and then pulled a small fur over her to keep the chill off.

"Goodnight, my sweet precious little bride. Oh how I look forward to the rest of our lives," he whispered as he laid a kiss on her shoulder before falling asleep.

Chapter Eleven
Proof

The smallest of taps woke Selrach. Light was seeping through a crack in the door. So he reached up and slid the door open ever so slightly. Mother's first woman was standing there, blocking the light. 'She is discreet if nothing else.'

Jannine still slept soundly, so he rose and rolled his side of the fur to reveal yet another. He then gently lifted her onto the clean fur. As he opened the door more widely and slid the roll out, Rewdan and Cirtap were waiting by Rewdan's door and step forward to take it from him. The maid then turned and handed him a large flask of tea and a bowl of food.

'Did she think of everything, or did mother?' He thought as he closed the door and tried to sleep once again. Unfortunately, his ears made him wait.

"My Lady, with all due respect, we can not present this to the people."

"And why not? It is her proof! She deserves to be recognized just as much as any other maiden bonded upon our land, foreigner or not."

"But my Lady, The people... they will not be able to see

anything."

"It is true My Lady... the black of the fur has absorbed any visual evidence. There is no color that remains!"

"Nonsense, they will see the glimmer of the morning sun upon the remaining dampness of her moisture."

"Moisture yes, but all know of your sons... endowment... and will expect to see more than mere moisture to recognize a legal bond with a pure bride."

"I have had enough of this. The people awake and begin to gather, the fur will be presented immediately and I will personally account for any whom wish to deny them due recognition as I was here last night... all night... and I heard her scream out for myself. If the fur is not proof enough, then the people will have my word as well as that of any Birthing Mistress who cares to examine the Plainsmaiden."

"Oh My Lady.... Oh, examinations should not be necessary, your word is more than enough."

"Oh Yes, certainly My Lady, My Queen. In Fact, if you would be so generous... I do believe that you should do the presentation yourself, to reaffirm that you personally bare witness to the event."

Footsteps could be heard as his mother snapped her fingers to the servants...

"Gentlemen, we all shall present her proof to the gathering."

"My love, who makes so much noise?"

He smiled and kissed her so warmly that she instinctively wrapped an arm around his neck before he whispered, "Our people cheer the future Queen. The Elders approved your offering and now present it to all that gather."

"What offering?"

"That blood which you granted me last night."

She sat up panicking and looked around. "Where are we? What happened to the black bear fur? Selrach?"

"Be calm my sweet. We are still within our chamber. Mother's first woman just brought us breakfast as I slipped out the offering."

"I don't understand? What offering?"

"The people seek proof of your virginity, your first blood is their proof, and as such I grant it to them as proof of the seal you kept unbroken for me. It is an old tradition. Any time a woman wishes to go down in history as a virgin bride, she must provide proof. Especially one new to our land. Don't you see? Now everyone will know how greatly you honor my family, your family, and me! Our bloodline has been blessed by your gift of first blood to me. You are now and forever more, my sole bride and heiress."

"I don't know whether to feel humiliated, or grateful."

"Why would you feel humiliated?"

"Now people will look at me and wonder how it was!"

"No more than any other couple after their first night."

"You don't think they heard us do you?"

"NO. I have never been so quiet."

"But did I not cry out?"

"Oh, that you did. If anyone was still awake during such a late hour, I doubt they would say anything but 'congratulations.'"

"Selrach, you mock me."

"Oh do promise you will do it again..."

"Surely."

"Good, I can't wait!"

He took the bread she was just putting in her mouth and ate it in one swallow as he smiled and pushed her against the door, kissing her until she giggled.

That, everybody heard. Garth, the ever-proud older brother, crept up the steps and opened the door. Selrach only half caught her as her nude body fell into her brother's arms, and Jannine screamed as all the brothers of the extended family burst out laughing. Mother of the wind helped her out so that she could stand while scolding the men, for apparently, her brother now had the Gift of Tongue of the Cliff Dwellers. Poor Jannine was left standing in the corner nude before all as she looked up at her man in disbelieving anger.

He, who had the fur of a bobcat about his waist, walked over and held it up around them both, still laughing, "Oh my sweet, do not be angry, it was an accident. Besides, we are all family here."

Jannine only turned her head in shame and wept on her mans' chest as the men stopped laughing and crowded around her, trying to apologize in her native Tongue to no avail. She was still naked and unbound. Not decent for them to lay eyes upon her. When she did not stop crying, Selrach gestured them to move away.

"My sweet, why do you cry?"

"My family is ignorant, and my man is an ingrate!" She spat, still frozen to his chest only half-covered by the fur, as her hair hid most of her body.

"Why would you call me such a thing on this of all days?"

"Because you would flaunt the gift of my flesh for other men to see."

She had him at that one. He himself had said how rare she was. The brothers looked to one another looking for help, as all were suddenly unable to speak. The silence calmed her and Selrach was offered a large elk fur by Rewdan who let it fall to the floor and wrapped the top about her shoulders. Selrach then tied the smaller of the two about his waist and swept his young bride up in his arms. This was the third time Cirtap had seen her this way and his brother was grateful to have someone around to help. So Cirtap took her in his arms long enough for Selrach to take the high seat. Then Jannine was laid upon his lap like a baby.

So close to the fire it grew quite hot inside the fur, but her pride would not allow her to make the first move.

"My sweet, how have you gotten by without me so long?"

She turned her head ever so slightly and saw Cirtap. Their eyes locked and he nodded his head.

"I think I know the answer to that," said Cirtap. "When I brought her back from her fall in the ocean, I personally undressed her to get her in the warm water more quickly. She had worn the same dress I first found her in as an under-dress. When we were traveling from pool to pool, she wore that same dress. Every night, she would crawl into bed fully dressed and emerge in the morning fully dressed. I don't think she has taken it off at all. Except for when she absolutely had to."

"You know, I think he is right," said Rewdan. "I remember how shocked I was to see the color of her arms when she walked on your back in the forest. She even wears a cloak when sitting by the fire."

"And last night my sweet, you did not remove your cloak until after you bid my kin good night."

"I saved myself for you!" she said.

Now he understood what an ingrate he really was. How uncomfortable she must have been. And what happened this morning! "Some how, I will find a way to make this up to you. I give you my word. You shall never feel so humiliated again." 'Humiliated! Oh how truly ignorant! And I thought the offering was a silly formality! I am off to a terrible start at being her man,' he thought.

"My love."

"Yes my sweet."

"Will you please take me back to our bedchamber?"

"Anything you want, my sweet."

"I just want to be alone in your arms."

'How can I be worthy of her flesh now?'

As he stood with her in his arms, he would hold her till the sun rose again, if that was what she desired. Fortunately, his arms were not all she wanted of him.

Chapter Twelve
The Giving of Thanks

Cirtap, he who had spent the most time with Jannine, was determined to make things right. His sister and future Queen must be made comfortable within their mother's house. After pacing in the entry for quite some time, he began to walk toward the storage building. There he walked from pile to pile. The Cliff Dwellers had abundant goods for trade of significant value, yet nothing struck him as a worthy gift for Jannine. After a while Primo became concerned about him, and so, went to Rewdan.

"My Lord, would you speak with me?" he asked.

"What lays on your mind Primo?"

"I am concerned about Cirtap's mind. He worries too much on matters as such should worry his brother instead."

Direct, but effective. He had Rewdan's complete attention.

"You speak of the matter between the future Queen and ourselves yet early this very morning?"

"I do."

"Where be my younger brother as we speak."

"He stalks the halls of collection, seeking answers."

"Speak no more of this and you will continue to serve him

honorably."

"Yes my Lord."

Primo nodded and quickly left the Long House feeling some sense of relief, for no sooner had he stood back on his own entry than did he turn around to see Rewdan and Garth walking toward the storage building.

"Brother, what thoughts plague your mind?" Rewdan asked when he found his brother leaning on the bottles of Seafaring whine.

"I keep seeing the tears on her face," said Cirtap. "I want her to feel as comfortable here as she did when I found her still dreaming of the home now forgotten," he mumbled as he stood there scratching his beard. "Some thing has pulled me here. The answer must lie within these walls, yet there has been so much trade between us and those of the Plains that there is more here of the Plains than there is anything else."

Garth nodded in agreement. He recognized many of his people's goods. Of course, his people traded many goods still in their infant form.

"I see what you mean," he said. "You have many pieces of our people and yet nothing complete. For example, that pile of fabric beside you. I can see a hundred different uses for all those different colors."

"Garth, you're a genius," exclaimed Rewdan.

"How so?" Asked Cirtap.

"This is the pile from the ship she came on. How happy do you think our brother would be to unwrap a new package every night?" Rewdan asked now holding a sample of green fabric as smooth as water in his hands.

"Such fabric as this would surly wear well on a Queen's shoulders." said Garth.

"And to think, I thought I might be loosing my mind!" Cirtap said in delight. "We must always speak among ourselves such as this, if we can make her cry tears of joy by tomorrow, together we can do anything."

"Dear brother, you over estimate us," said Rewdan. "Together we can lead our people to accomplish anything. It will take the hands of many women if we are to craft these into dresses by tomorrow."

"Than we must summon them now," Cirtap laughed as he walked

to the door.

Mother was most pleased with their plan, and sent three of her housemaids to gather more. Primo, still without children, offered his house for the day's work. By the end of the day, more than half the village women were hard at work. Some sewing, some embroidering. A girl as slender as Jannine was placed on a stool so that they could guess her size more accurately, and all three men supervised the remainder of the day.

They had decided to have several dresses made in one day. All of different colors, but with the same details. Each dress would be synched down the back so that only their brother could untie it in the dark. Every one that looked at her would merely see cloth tightly wrapped around her bound by invisible cords. The fabric was cut large enough to fit even after she became heavy with child (as they all hoped it would come soon). No matter what her size, the cords upon her back would draw tight to her.

Each gown was made with three layers. The longest of which would be made of white silk and would line her body within. The finest dyed outer layer, would have gold embroidery about the bodice and feet signifying that only the King may tread between. Each gown would also be accompanied by a matching short cloak. This would cover her chest, neck and arms. As a finishing touch, the young girl who had stood all day long offered some cording of braided fabric. These were just long enough to bind the hair that would also be kept for the King. The eldest women worked late into the night securing the last stitches of the golden crowns.

In the morning, every member of the community could feel pride in the Lady's new clothes, as they were truly a community effort that would show their skills to the world. As the sun broke the horizon, the Queen accompanied her head woman to Primo's house. There they found the green dress laid upon a stack of folded gowns, all tied like packages. They looked like folded fabric secured by cordage. One of a pale pink, one of the purest white, one the shade of the red earth, one the color of the sky after a fire, and one the color of the setting sun after a rain. There was one the color of a small purple flower native to the

Cliffs, and two that resembled the sun on dried fields. Including the one she held of the deepest green available by the trees, there were nine total. Primo and Garth dressed early that morning and helped carry the offering to the Long House.

Such a sight it would be for months to come. Never had a woman had so many dresses. Most of the women had no more than three. One for working in the cold, one for working in the heat, and one kept nice for feasting within the Long House. Their Lady would have three times that, and none for working.

Once they arrived, Cirtap and Rewdan rose to inspect them immediately. All agreed that they were more than worthy, but they had to be presented properly. Cirtap took control of that. The two dresses resembling the moody sky were placed on his seat as he had traveled with her and assisted in her purification. The two dresses resembling the sun on dried fields, he gave to Garth, as he was her brother and Prince of the Plains People. The dress of pure white and the dress of red earth went to his mother, as she represented both mothers. Rewdan was to give her the dresses resembling pink and purple flowers. The green dress, to hopefully bring fertility, was left aside still unwrapped as they hoped she would wear it as often as she liked (even today).

Mother was then sent to bring forth her son.

For the second time in as many days, a tap woke Selrach with Jannine still in his arms. He lifted his head and cracked the door. His mother saw the light on their heads and spoke softly so as not to wake his bride.

"We would have a word with you before she rises Selrach."

"What for?"

"Just come. I believe your brothers have found a way for you to please your bride outside of your bedchamber."

"I'll be right there."

He was almost ecstatic as he pulled his leggings on. 'What could it be?'

In the last few days he had come to be surprised in so many ways, and yet he had a new appreciation of how insightful his brothers could be. He had already dressed himself and only disturbed her when he reached for the door.

"Selrach?"

"Hush my sweet; I just rise to let my water."

She rolled over to where he had laid and breathed of his smell within the warm fur as he opened the door and backed out only to have his brothers lay their hands upon his eyes. They turned him around and shut the door, then walked him over to the high bench. Using words of the Tongue of the Cliff Dwellers, Rewdan started speaking first.

"Dear brother, I want you to travel in your mind to the day before this and think of how I laid a fur upon you while you held your tearful bride."

"I thought mother said you would help me please my bride, not bring forth such a terrible memory."

"Dear brother, think back farther and tell us, with the knowledge you now hold, how would you have liked to emerge with your bride?" Cirtap said.

"She would be smiling, holding my hand and wearing the finest gown that covered her from neck to toe. Such a gown that no man ever dare lift but me..."

"Then congratulate us for being brilliant leaders of the greatest people in all the four lands," laughed Rewdan.

They released their hands and Selrach saw Garth holding a heavy long green gown with gold embroidery.

"Congratulations indeed, such craftsmanship must have taken all day and all night."

"Half the village women in fact. We decided that she should have enough to wear a different gown each day to show not only how much you can give her, but also how much she can give you!"

"Don't tell her that, she doesn't like that people think of what we share."

They all smiled. If it were not for her still sleeping only feet away, they would have laughed out loud. "Please, brother dear. Has bonded life yet been good to you at all?"

"Promise not to tell?"

"Promise" they all said in unison.

"My bride, for as meek and humble as she may seem, has such

fire within her that not only did she take ALL that I had to give on her first try, but has awoken him and embraced him so many times since, that I am glad to say that I could have no need of another woman so long as I live."

"You jest," said Garth. "I would be ever so proud, but she is such a little thing!"

"Not so little that he does not grow within," said Selrach. "Do not say whether you believe me or not; instead, wait and see for yourself how it now pains her to spread her legs, or take pressure on her rump. Yet still she smiles and asks for more. The fire within her wants more than her flesh can bear," the pride showed in his eyes and gratitude covered the twinge of hunger in his voice.

"She may need to return home then," said Garth.

"She is home," said Selrach.

"Many women of the Plains have been known to grow so thin and gaunt in foreign lands, as to make them barren. I saw her during her fifteenth harvest. Though very slender, her bones did not show as they do now. The memory of the sight of her bones worries me. I have known my share of women of the Plains, and none so frail looking as she," said Garth.

"Let us not jump to such fretful thoughts. Let me instead fill her with love all this long winter. She shall do nothing but eat, sleep and keep my bed. If she still does not gain in body, then we can talk of travel in the spring," said Selrach.

"I think that is very wise brother. Perhaps even the lovers pool may help," offered Cirtap.

"Think me not suspicious, but I am curious as to why you would mention such a place knowing where you have recently been." Selrach said with a smile.

Cirtap blushed and scratched is head, "It is just that she was so strong on that journey. She truly soaked in the water like roots of a mighty tree. Besides, you have nothing to suspect. I am no fool. I know she closed her eyes only to pray that it was you who could have been the one to present and purify her."

"If I am to ever take her for a swim, I must get her dressed and fed."

"Let us make a wall for her. The first time you put one of these on her, you will need the light," said mother.

Garth handed Selrach the green dress, which he laid on the floor next to his door. Then each of his brothers grabbed a fur and their stack of dresses. With their mother helping them, they held the gifts behind the furs. With one hand each, they held up three furs between the four of them.

Selrach then opened the door and kissed his bride, "Jannine my sweet, I have something for you."

"Any time you desire my lord," she whispered.

Chuckles could be heard as she looked passed her man at the furs hanging beyond.

"I will remember your offer, but that is not what I had in mind."

She curled back up and grabbed the fur they had slept on.

"You must trust me this morning. I promise you will like what my brothers have prepared. They wish to apologize for the misunderstanding yesterday. They went to our people while we shared the day together, and asked them to prepare an offering in return. The whole village worked late into the night, just to see you smile as the future Queen should. Please come out to me, and trust enough to leave the fur behind. Just this once, grant me what I ask of you."

Jannine got that look of determination on her face, closed her eyes and slowly let him pull her out to stand before him, still too scared to look. When he stepped back to pick up the dress, she reached out and called to him. "Selrach, please tell me what you are doing?"

He held back a laugh and said, "Now I need you to pray as if my mother was flying above you and you wished to reach her in the sky."

She lifted her arms and tilted her head up, allowing her hair to fall down her back as Selrach gathered the fabric and dropped it over her. It must have felt cool for she shivered as it unfolded. A moment later, she opened her eyes to see smooth green fabric on her breast that fell all the way to the floor. Selrach was behind her pulling a cord that made the fabric tighten on her ribs, then waist and hips. No further, for now she was with her man.

She then turned and looked him in the face and again began to cry, "It is so beautiful Selrach."

"I'm not done yet," he said.

He combed her hair and wound it, then tied a knot securing it in place with the braided fabric. He then kissed her neck goodbye before he put the small cloak about her shoulders, "Now no man may ever look upon you thinking you are anything but mine."

When she was finally allowed to move, she reached up and wrapped her arms around his neck and kissed him through her tears.

"Who else so deserves my thanks today?" she asked as he laughed and pushed her back down.

The furs dropped and she saw the faces of her new family. Each one holding more fabric. She turned to her mother, untied the white fabric on top, and gasped when it unfolded and dropped to the floor while still in her hands. "Oh Selrach, if only I had had this on the day you arrived." He couldn't help but think what a sight that would have been.

"This one we must save then," he said. "I wish to see this one on you every time I return home."

"Oh Selrach!" She kissed him again then hugged and kissed everyone present, then ran to the door with out any shoes or her mother's cloak. Selrach ran and caught her at the door.

"What are you doing?"

"I wish to thank them."

"All right, but not beyond the entry, it is snowing again."

She burst through the doors to find that only a few stable boys were out.

"Ask them to come here Selrach."

"You there, stable boys. My bride wishes a word with you."

They looked at each other, then came running. She looked like something out of a dream as she spoke to the future King.

"My bride bids you to tell the village that we will feast in the Long House every night until the skilled craftsman have enjoyed the sight all her new gifts, with the exception of that which she will save for when I return from my many future trips."

The boys looked at each other again, "Eight nights of feasting! We shall be fat before winter ends!"

"Well, off with you."

They scattered, and in a few moments, people stood on their entries waving furiously at them. Selrach held his bride about her dainty waist as she blew kisses across the courtyard. After a while, he had had enough and swept her off her feet to carry her within again. Men would remark how precious she must have been for all he could do was smile while waiting to have her alone again, while all they saw of her were her hands, face, and a toe that peaked from beneath her skirts when he carried her within. Some of the jealous women only remarked that it is not so humble to be adorned in so many rich fabrics. They were easily dismissed by the men and reminded that they did not care how something was wrapped so long as what the wrapping held was worthy and theirs alone.

Feast they did, and every night, Jannine walked up and down the hall till every last one of them were ready for bed, always carrying a pitcher of water and a pitcher of beer. She never stopped smiling, and only sat when her man put food in her mouth. By the second night, word of the new bride had traveled to other villages; and thus, the Queen had more food to prepare than ever before. Some village leaders predicted how exceedingly large the gathering would become and opened their halls so that only those living in their village would stay for the full eight nights. When the feasting came to an end, Jannine had earned a place of respect among the Cliffs Dwellers. More than half of their people would travel through the snow to meet the future Queen, and all who did would agree she was more than worthy of the future King.

Chapter Thirteen
The Lovers Pool

After two full moons had come and gone, Jannine emerged yet again from the woman's house. She had spent the last four days bleeding in solitude, as none of the other women in the village spoke the Tongue of the Plains People. Most were so modest as her as to be unable to acquire it, so they were learning to read each other's body language instead. Jannine learned how they took turns with the chores and had already assumed certain duties within the house. She fed the fire, made tea, prepared fresh cloth and even helped to clean that which was soiled. Only the Queen heard of such tasks and was pleased to hear that although showing no sign of fertility, Jannine was working her fair share when ever possible.

Jannine however, never wanted the pains to come, but was grateful for time among her peers. For Selrach had been insistent that the future Queen should have no need of learning remedial tasks, and thusly, the winter had been rather empty and long. In the meantime, Selrach enjoyed her daylight misery though, as she was full of life every night by the light of their candle.

On this day, she emerged to find herself blinded by the morning sun. Her mothers' cloak lay in her arms as she lifted her skirts to step down off the porch of the Women's House. Selrach was just emerging himself and smiled to see her once again. So she paused and lowered her skirts. Selrach then ran across the courtyard and smiled even more as she fell into his arms.

"Where shall I carry you today, my sweet?"

"I think my prayer has been answered."

"What prayer is that?"

"The one I sent to the sun asking for him to return just once before spring arrived."

"Why would you have need of the sun? Do I not warm you enough?"

"Indeed, my Lord. I just wanted to go for a ride with you before you left for the Trade Season."

Selrach had not yet told her that she would be coming with him. Even though he had been making her eat twice as much food as any other woman, she still showed no signs of a child, and remained as thin as the day when he had first arrived home. Even his mother and the council of Elders agreed that the King would have to make his home on the Plains.

"Some time has passed since Cirtap last spoke of it but I do believe he knew the perfect destination for our ride."

"Oh Selrach, he knows me well. Please tell me what place he spoke of."

"It is a place for lovers to enjoy the sun, even in the middle of winter. By horseback, it is not far at all. We should be there in time for the midday meal."

He set her down on a dry spot on the barn floor, then saddled her horse for her. He then went to saddle his own. When he turned back to help her up, he saw her lying across her horses back trying to swing her leg over. She slid off and stood back to straighten her skirts as he asked, "What exactly was that?"

She looked at him innocently and said, "I seem to have forgotten how to mount with abundant skirts about my legs."

"Only Plainsmen hunters mount bareback that way," he exclaimed.

"Really?" she said.

"That explains why she is such a good shot," said one of the guards.

"Explain yourself man."

"I'm sorry my lord, I should not have said anything, Primo was bid by my lord Cirtap to swear us to silence."

"No wonder you did not ask me to heal your back after carrying the fire wood," exclaimed Jannine.

The guard only blushed and excused himself, leaving them alone with the horses.

"Does this have something to do with when you got this horse?"

Now it was Jannine's turn to blush, "Yes my Lord."

"I see."

"You are not angry... are you?"

"Jannine, if I am to become King of all four lands, there will be many battles. Some planned, and some not. I hate to think of you in the middle of bloodshed, so it does give me strength to know that you can hold tight to reins. Perhaps we may even send for a forging. There may come a time when you may have need of a sword on your side."

"If I am half as good with a blade as I am with a bow, my Lord shall have nothing to trouble his dreams."

'She is so confident.' His Curiosity made him wish for spring while he silently hoped that she would never use a bow for anything but sport. "Come, let me help you up. As soon as we get a basket, we can ride."

He led her up the hill beyond the unused signal fire and deep into the woods. From time to time, she kicked her horse to a gallop and they played tag in the trees. He loved how sporting she was, so full of life and absolutely fearless.

"It is just around the bend," he shouted as he passed her yet again.

He had said that before and this time she no longer believed him until her horse walked passed his. She only stopped when she saw him lighting a torch with some stones from his saddle bags.

"This will signify to all who pass, that the pool is occupied."

He kicked his horse and it jumped across a stream falling over a cliff. There he lit another torch. Her horse paralleled his up stream until he lit another and crossed back to light the one at her side. Together they silently entered the smallest of canyons.

Selrach dismounted and led the horses between some trees, following a stream strangled by two mighty pine trees. When she realized the rocks allowed no breeze to enter, she let her mother's cloak fall off her back. If not for the sun enveloping the sky that reached from rock face to rock face, it would have felt like a cave. Just within the trees, there was a small patch of grass, still green and free of snow. (The horses were all too happy to stand and eat their fill as long as allowed.) Within, the sun shone off walls made of smooth rocks, eaten away by water. In the middle she saw nothing but mist surrounded by small plants she had never seen before. They seemed to connect the mist and the rock, like a green chain about the neck.

Selrach removed his fur Cloak and laid it on some small rounded pebbles then took off his shoes and shirt. He then came to his bride and pulled her shoes off as well. Only after placing them on the cloak did he finally lift her down.

"Selrach, the grass is not even cold."

"The water will be even warmer."

Selrach removed her small cloak and admired her smooth pale skin. Then he whispered as he kissed her and wrapped his arms tightly around her waist, lifting her to him. He could tell she was already responding when her knee lifted to the side and then her bare foot hooked behind his knee.

"Shall you take what I have already?"

She looked down and only smiled as her fingers untied the top of his leggings. Then she took him by the hand and led him to the cloak.

"No," she said at last. "Not yet. I'm too hungry to 'Take.'"

She was still smiling when he sat down beside her and watched her open the basket to find a wide assortment of sweet things to eat.

"Such a delightful bounty. Your mother must want me round before your child begins to grow."

"Not so round, just enough to sustain my weight without so much noise. I always think I'm hurting you."

Suddenly, she turned and looked at him with a twinkle in her eye.

"I hate that you would think such a thing. Tell me, does this really sound like hurting?" Jannine had his full attention as she placed a tart into her mouth, closed her eyes and slowly began to chew. As the fruit dissolved on her tongue, she slumped to the side and started to moan.

'Is she telling me that that is how she shows pleasure?' Selrach thought, already becoming aroused.

She took up another tart and placed it in his mouth. Instead of swallowing it whole like he normally would, he too slowly chewed it allowing the fruit within to dissolve on his tongue. The flavor was as consuming as the blood within a large piece of meat cooked slowly within the earth. Therefore, he could not help but let a small moan escape his lips as well.

Jannine smiled at the thought of exploiting a new found weakness in her man and moved the basket closer to him. He fed her another, she fed him and he leaned back on the rock face, chewing as slowly as he could stand. When he swallowed, she was waiting with another at his lips. When he opened his mouth she placed it on his tongue as she sat upon his lap. He smiled as he chewed and she felt something begin to grow below her skirts. So she lifted that which lay between them before he pulled her hips upon his.

When she leaned forward to place a kiss on his lips, she let out another moan as he penetrated deeply within her. When she caught her breath and opened her eyes, he had another tart ready for her lips. She smiled and bit it in half, delivering the other half to his mouth. As she held her lips to his, so as to match his jaw chew for chew, she began to breathe deeply and pull with her hips keeping the same rhythm. His hands began holding her firmly as he dug his fingers unto the cloth of her dress hiding all that he now felt riding him. Selrach soon found himself closing his eyes and envisioned her by candlelight doing the exact same thing. In his minds eye, he saw her breast, he saw the muscles of her belly move, he saw her ribs rise and fall. Eventually, Selrach opened his eyes and looked into her face. She only blinked now and then, ever watchful of his response.

"You grow silent my sweet," he whispered.

"He has found his home and settled within," she replied as she continued to rock and sway.

The pressure was just enough to stay him longer. "Do you wish to sleep my sweet?" he asked out of mere jest.

"Not till every star in the sky shines my love."

She smiled as he pulled her so close as to force breath from her lungs, then bent forward and left a hot mark on the small amount of breast showing above the top of her dress. He then grabbed his blade and went to cut the straps that bound her dress.

"Selrach, No!"

"I just want to cut a cord."

"But it was a gift of your people... and how will I get home?"

"Oh woman, even in the heat of passion you dare deny me?"

He was actually angry at her! How could that be? His poor bride looked as much shocked as scared.

"Never my Lord"

"Don't ever call me that. Not when we are as close as this. I am your Man, not your Master. Anything I may become, will be because of you. Today I am a Prince of one land and you are my bride, a Princess in your own right. Do not ever relent to anyone. Not even me," he demanded as he grabbed hold of her hips and made an extra firm point of it.

She gasped and smiled again as she thought aloud, "But what if I want to yield to you?"

"The only thing I want yielding to me, is that which I hunt."

"Promise?"

He put both of his hands on his heart and bowed his head, "I Promise".

She giggled, put her hands on his shoulders and then jumped away. He was on his feet in no time and caught her only a few feet away only to have her slip down and out of his arms.

"Damn such fine fabric and damn you for being so slim," he shouted, causing her to laugh and kick some water at him. "Oooo you really are asking for trouble aren't you?"

"Nope! No trouble at all."

In that instant, her fate was sealed. For every two steps he took toward her, she took one back. When he sprinted, he had her before she could run. He had caught her by hooking his arm around her waist and lifting her off the ground, so he used his other hand to untie the single cord on her back. Jannine was kicking furiously, and even went so far as to punch him on the back. Selrach merely laughed at the thought of her trying to hurt him and dropped her to the ground. At the feel of grass beneath her feet, Jannine instantly jumped and tried to run, but her dress had fallen just enough to trip her, allowing him to fall on her, laughing as her arms struggled to keep her dress about her.

"Now what do you have to say for yourself, do you yield?" He declared in his most triumphant voice.

"You haven't caught me yet."

"Oh I haven't, have I?" He gave the dress a jerk and it was down to her knees. Jannine kicked it free and ran to the water, diving to safety.

When she was finally treading water some distance away, she laughed and shouted to her man, "My love, when will you fulfill your promise? I tire of this game. I thought a man of your standing would be a finer hunter than that," she mocked as she leaned back, exposing her breasts and belly, then kicked water at him with such aim that his chest got wet.

"Ooh woman, how you bring me to heat. Would you make an animal of me?"

"I would at that. An animal swift as the wind, strong as the earth, and as passionate as the sea."

"Would you have me also deliver my seed as an animal?"

"Only if it pleases you to take such hold of me."

At these words, Selrach dropped his pants and strode out into the water. As he was taller than she was, he could stand easily while she had her arms spread to help her stay afloat. As a ruse, he also swayed and waved his arms in the water. "Do you yield now?"

"No"

'This is going to be fun,' he thought as he exaggerated and took a deep breath, dropping his head into the water.

She kicked and screamed while turning. Just to taunt her, he reached over to tickle her feet. She jumped to the side. He tickled the other foot and she jumped over him. Just as he wanted! He then stood with her legs about his face, causing Jannine to scream as he lifted her high above the water. She was stuck, with her belly about his face and he loved it. He lifted her even higher still and kissed that which only he knew, causing her to moan. His hand supported her back (not allowing her to fall) while her legs curled around his neck and her fingers gripped his scalp. Her fluid was flowing as heavy as the stream.

"Do you yield?"

"Yesss"

Finally, he let her fall into the water and pulled her hips toward him. Only her arms and head remained above the water, when he was finally within her yet again. Her legs helped her to rise and fall as she could contain her hunger no longer.

"Shhhh, I have caught you and now I shall have you," Selrach whispered.

Jannine opened her eyes to look up in his face, to see an expression that she was not familiar with, as Selrach carried her out of the water and laid her upon his cloak.

"I have tasted my victory, now I wish to hear you scream," he declared as he rose to kneel and pulled her legs to his chest. He then took hold of her hips and drove them home. Again and again he pounded her with the fury of the tides. Again and again she reached for him. Never did he relent until such fury and speed caused her to send forth a scream that echoed beyond the canyon. Then and only then did he finish and leave his seed dripping from her spring before he laid his head upon her chest and breathed deeply of her flesh while watching her legs quivering at his side.

"Promise to please me so greatly as this every time I return to you!"

"Return from where?"

"The Women's House."

"I hope you don't mind, but I think I would like to more often than that."

"Even when we are old?"

"I hope so. My uncle is now gray, and still so strong as to take a third bride that I heard scream like that just last spring."

"Will you make a third bride scream?"

"Only if you had same-birth sisters," he looked up to see her smile and began to think she might sleep. "Please tell me you do not feel drowsy. I have four whole days and nights worth of that waiting for you."

"Would you mind so much if I rested before receiving it all?"

"Rest you may, but not till I am also ready to rest."

She smiled and stroked the hair of his arm.

"Your seed has taken my resistance away. Selrach, my hunter, you may take all you please."

"Than I shall purify you and begin anew."

Selrach took his flesh so stealthily won, back to where he had caught her. He sat with her on his lap and poured handfuls of water all over her body, until all that remained above the surface of the water glistened in the sun. He then carried her out to where he had stood before. His left arm guided her so that she floated next to his chest, allowing his right hand to caress the rest of her within the water. When he finally returned to his favorite place, her hips sank ever so slightly to open to him. He caressed the folds and the opening they held. She moaned as he found a spot more tender than the rest, he began to rise again as she continued to moan.

'This could never be considered purification,' he thought as she reached for his hand and pulled on his arm. "What do you want my sweet?"

"You said you meant to purify me. I do not feel purified within."

"What do you feel?"

"I feel, I feel... It is like the flame has been relit."

"The flame of hunger?"

"Hunger. Hunger for more. Hunger for more within."

Curiosity got the better of him, and he sank two fingers within. She let out a cry, more than a moan and less than a scream. Never had he felt within so. In a moment he found the spot he had pushed forth that made her scream, and bent both fingers up with firm pressure. Her free arm splashed in the water as her eyes rolled back in her head.

'If she bites any harder, she will cause her own lip to bleed.'

He did it again and a heavy groan burst from those lips.

"Selrach."

He removed his hand and pulled her hips down on him. So clean were her folds that he had a fight to push through and in.

"Ahh!"

She scratched his neck and she pulled his hair as there was nothing else for her to hold on to.

"Oh Selrach..."

He stopped pushing so hard and slid his hands up to her waist, pulling her dainty ribs up to his chest. Jannine opened her eyes and stared at him, then kissed his lips and sought out his tongue. He had longed for this for so long that he sucked in her tongue until she sucked back on his. Such passion, such hunger, as he had nurtured within her caused her to wrap her arms around his head as she could no longer resist tapping into his mind and drawing on the essence of his deepest desires. There she saw herself kissing him, through his eyes, as he had wished... countless times.

As her breath became cold, his hands released their hold on her. Her cold breath in return was filled with disappointment as she begged, "Don't stop. I can take it all. Give me your seed. Make me grow large. Force me to bring forth your son. Don't stop, not ever, I swear I am strong enough to take it all..."

Such a sweet new accent had taken over her voice... as if out of his dreams... as a reward, he sucked on her neck so hard that she screamed again and released her grip, giving him the opportunity to drive it all home. The pressure was so great that she hardly felt him shudder, but he did not withdraw until he knew she could stand no more pleasure and still come back for more under the sun; as Jannine went limp on his shoulder, they sank back into the water. Selrach rinsed his hair and could not help but smile at the thought of his brother's faces when she would join in conversation at dinner tonight. He would not yet tell her that she had taken his tongue. If she knew, she might never speak it in public and he knew as well as any that all his people (including his mother) had been praying every night that he might awaken such a flame within her soon.

Yet his fingers still remembered how smooth and tight the child's door within had been. He would open that door. Even if she had to travel half the world. He would make his seed take bed. This he also would not speak of. Only his mother would know. Perhaps a woman of her years and skill would know of an herb that would help.

Chapter Fourteen
Powers of Persuation

The sun was yet still high as they floated to the shallows. He lifted his head to drain water from his ears just in time to see a rather portly man walking toward him.

"You there, come no further!"

The man stopped and raised a hand up to shield his eyes from the sun. Half blind from working in the mines, he did not see Selrach kneeling in the water. He turned and looked behind him and saw no one there either.

"Hello," came the scared voice of the old man.

"Why do you enter the sacred valley of the well?" asked Selrach. Jannine was alert now and hiding behind him.

"Who asks these questions?"

"A man with his young bride!"

"I do apologize, I could not see the flames by daylight. I beg your pardon for I must gather a pail of water."

"What for?"

"The messenger from the Queen swore me to secrecy before the first heavy snow came. I could only tell you now if you took my life. Oh please do not for it will leave us with out a King."

"Why would you say such a thing?"

"Please do not ask of me what I cannot answer."

Jannine rose and grabbed her mother's cloak off her horse. Selrach watched in amazement as she hugged it to her chest and approached the man. She waved her hand before his face. He did not blink.

"Is somebody there?"

"Old man, you have traveled too far for one of your age, so I tell you now, do not fear me for I am the most honored guest of the Queen. Please, tell me. I will not have your life and nor will my man. Rather, the Queen would have the life of he that would take it from me," Jannine spoke in words soft as the breeze.

"Oh dear sweet Lady. You are too kind to me. When the virgin bride returned to the mountain, I was bid to draw the metal from the mud. The sacred water was used to craft the most powerful sword in our entire world for the coming High King. Word is, he bears his bride very well, so well indeed that there is talk that he may yet awaken a flame so strong that even the purest of virgin brides may soon take forth his Gift of Tongue. I have completed his sword and now seek this water that I may wrap his handle in the finest, smoothest leather I can find."

"What all do you need for the leather?"

"Water of love will have to do."

"If you could soak the leather in anything, what would you have?"

"I would have that which flows from his bride. Urine can make leather turn white as the sky and soft to the touch."

Jannine put her hand on his that held the bucket.

"My lady?"

"Grant me the bucket and I will fetch your water."

He let go and she took it to the water. She filled the bucket just shy of the top then sat upon it and let her water flow. She then walked back and returned it to his hand.

"When shall you deliver it to the Queen?"

"Does the moon yet shine?"

"The moon first showed last night and will begin to smile tomorrow."

"Good. I hope to send it with a messenger by the next full

moon."

"Will you not come?"

"My lady, my body only knows the paths within the caves. I dare not travel beyond the stream where I gather strength every day, as the stream provides me fresh water every morning. It is just for the future King that I dare come between the trees."

"Then I will thank you now," she whispered, as she leaned over the balding man and placed a kiss on the top of his head.

"Oh my lady, if only the future King could receive a kiss such as that."

"I have, several times, and intend to every day we are within reach till the day I die. Now off with you man, for you shall not receive another. Say not a word of our meeting and you shall receive a fine gift indeed when my mother thinks she has surprised me."

"Yes My Lord."

The terrified little man instantly turned and reached for the trees. When he had found his place again, he walked off at a good pace, and was out of sight before Selrach stood by his bride.

"How comes it to be that he would tell you and not me?"

"He was no threat. As I knew he would not harm me, I let him have nothing to fear as well."

"You made him let down his guard!"

"Tell me Selrach... How does a man of your caves come to know my Tongue?"

"Because the prayers of our people were answered."

"What do you mean?"

"Our love awoke such a flame within you, that burned for me. I heard you begging in the Tongue you had finally taken from me, and help me so, I want to hear it again," just to toy with her, he had changed from Plains Tongue to Cliff Tongue as he spoke, wrapping his arms around her once again.

Her eyes became as big around as was possible. Then her jaw dropped as she tried to pull away, "Selrach, no. It can't be. I only wish to be worthy."

"Silly woman, this makes you even more worthy. You took it from me while I gladly gave you all I have and while planting my seed.

When you speak to our people, in the Tongue of my people, they will know how badly you want to give me a child. They will know that the bloodline continues within you."

She was biting her lip again, and he sucked it from her as they fell to their knees once again.

When the sun fell beyond the rocks, they knew their time had come and gone. She redressed and he helped her to mount. For the ride home, she would ride sidesaddle. He smiled to himself at the thought that she could finally take no more as he led the horses out and gathered water in his hands from the stream to douse the flames. They then rode home in silence, enjoying what serenity the forest could give before returning to the bustle of the Queen's Village.

When they reached the Long House, he lifted her directly to the entry. Rewdan and Cirtap were waiting. Thinking themselves cunning they continued to speak as they had been in the Tongue of their birth.

"See how she rides. I can almost feel her pain," said Cirtap

"So much pain must mean a day of pleasure. See how she looks at him longingly. Our brother must have used his tongue on more than one of her openings," said Rewdan.

"You only wish," said Cirtap.

"Oh if only, as if you don't," said Rewdan

"One day, when I find a woman worthy, you shall be standing here listening to her voice echoing out of the mountain."

"Dear brother, did it hurt your little man, or just your ears?" asked Rewdan.

"Neither," said Jannine. "In fact, he promised to do the same every time I come back from the women's house. If not more often than that," she smiled as she walked passed them and through the open door.

Garth had just come out when they arrived and heard the whole thing. "Ooh Weee! She got you good! Man, am I ever glad I wasn't a part of that. Selrach, my brother, I will be thanking you every time I laugh tonight, and tomorrow, and the next day. Ah ha ha ha ha"

"That was pretty good, wasn't it..." said Selrach

Chapter Fifteen
Dan

Garth entered the hall behind Selrach laughing so hard that the entire assembly went quiet. Jannine took a seat just shy of the Queen, allowing room for her man. Garth sat at her side, still laughing so hard that tears flowed from his eyes. Finally, Rewdan and Cirtap took their seat on the other side of their mother.

The Queen passed her first born a platter and asked, "What has gotten into our guest?"

"He enjoys the spirit within my bride."

"What surprises has she in store for us today?" asked the Queen.

"She merely expresses intolerance of my brothers' rude behavior as would befit my bride."

"Shall I not hear more?"

"I merely put an end to their game," Jannine said, in the Tongue of the Cliff Dwellers.

"That is good to hear. You must tell me more while we sip our evening tea."

"That would truly be a pleasure my Queen," said Jannine

That night, she talked to everyone who could find an excuse to approach the royal family. Selrach was more than pleased to see her face aglow when a little girl showed her a doll wearing a gown of left over pink fabric. Even some little boys took the opportunity to swear allegiance to her, bragging of how they would fight for her honor when they grew up. Jannine was even entranced by one of the Village Elders who told her a tale of how their tradition of providing proof began. Jannine just soaked it all in. She took to speaking the Tongue of the Cliff Dwellers as if she had been born to it and was so grateful to no longer be living among strangers.

When Jannine finally learned which child had been Blossom's, she remembered his face and asked for his name, Dan. She then waited till all had gone and kissed her man goodnight. This was finally her chance to talk to her mother in-law.

"The Lovers Pool was good to my children today," said the Queen.

"Very good indeed. One might say there was magic in the water."

"One could at that."

"Mother, I have been hoping that you could tell me more of what happened to my mother."

"Her gifts, her death, even her travels... These things have been told to you."

"Yes, but it is not the same. You knew her. You lived with her. You watched her grow. I want to know what she was like, what pieces of her may lay within me."

"She was a woman of quiet determination. This, I have seen in you. You remind me of her when you study people as if trying to read their soul. I expect you will gain her talent for judging the heart of people. She could always tell a person's intentions. You also have her hope and her sincerity. You will always be good to my son. I could tell when I saw you crying the morning of the day he would arrive. You were so concerned about what he would want, what he would need, even require of you. I don't know that it is possible for you to put yourself first, but I must tell you to try to learn. Selrach will not always be able to get you what you want. There are some things you will have to acquire for yourself. Much as you did today. When my son is traveling, it will be your place to keep the fires lit. You will host dinners. You will speak with guests. You must learn to gather knowledge, as that will prove to be the most powerful weapon of all. If I had not known to gather knowledge from you when I first saw you, you would not be alive, and my son may never have returned to me and the prophecy would remain unfulfilled for another generation. If you wish to finish the work that your mother started, you must be ever more vigilant than I," the Queen finished speaking and could tell Jannine had taken heed of every word.

"Mother, there is something that bothers me."

"Speak freely my child."

"Cirtap had a son by the woman Blossom."

"Yes, he is watched by the family of one of the guards."

"He will know what his mother did."

"When he is older, yes."

"When will he know his father?"

"What do you mean?"

"If Cirtap does not raise him, what will he think when he becomes a man? If a child is unworthy of love... Whether she was worthy or not, Dan still carries your blood. Why is he not made welcome?"

"Do you fear him following his mother's path?"

"I see he is destined to misunderstand unless Cirtap accepts him without blame."

"You are wise to bring this up with me. Perhaps I should ask the Elders for advice in this matter."

"When the men leave in the spring, I would like the opportunity to speak with the boy."

"That would be difficult."

"How so?"

"I am not certain that Selrach would accept him into your house."

"What house am I to have?"

"The one he will build for you on the land of your birth. My dear Jannine, I fear you are still so weak as you are so far from the land that flows in your blood. If you are to conceive my grandchildren, it will be within your own four walls."

"Then why would Selrach have a say in the child Dan."

"Cirtap will be spending much of his time with you on the Plains as he is Captain of the Guard."

"If you would speak to the Elders, I would speak with my man and my brother."

"I can see that it weighs heavily on you, so I will speak with them tomorrow. In the mean time, my son still waits."

"If only your sons had your grace."

"Grace is often something left to women; this is why the prophecy is of unions."

She gave mother of the wind a kiss on the cheek before silently stepping up to their bedchamber door.

As she crawled in beside him, Selrach asked, "Have you had your fill of my mother's wisdom tonight?"

"You had not yet told me that I would be leaving with you in the spring."

"We had not yet decided if you would go on the first trip of the season, so I thought I would make it a surprise. Does this have anything to do with my brother's son? I heard mention of his name."

"I am worried for his future. Without his mother, he will need his father more if he is to be led on a path more befitting his father's blood."

Jannine had chosen these words most carefully and hoped it would work.

"Are you saying we should take him in?"

"I would make him welcome. I would have him raised to see the honorable man he has of a father. I would have him raised in a home where he was not a pitied orphan, but family. Considering the circumstances of his mother's death, I fear he may need the guidance of his blood more than ever."

"For a woman of your years, who had been so near death by that woman's hands, I never would have expected this."

"Don't you see, she acted rashly because she had no security. Cirtap would not bond with her, his child is yet unclaimed, she had nothing in life but hope. When she saw me in Cirtap's arms, fear made her see red. I do not want Dan's eyes to be so clouded by doubt."

"You are right. I will tell my brother to make a house for him in the spring. He will live here comfortably."

"You misunderstand. I wish for him to look forward to his father's return. I wish for him to bear witness to his father's victories and woes. Will you please grant this to me? Please, let it be me that speaks with Cirtap," she asked.

He smiled at her twinkling eyes. She had the gift of tact his mother was known for. "As you wish, I will ask him to let you ride along with him tomorrow. He intends to ride the coast, double checking the caves with half the guard."

At breakfast, Jannine sat silent, unable to find any words.

Cirtap noticed how she seemed distant. Not once had she met his eyes. Something was not right, and then he knew what.

"So, how long do you expect your ride to take today?" asked Selrach.

"Not so long, I have told my men to eat a hearty breakfast so that we can continue to ride through the midday meal."

Jannine picked up a large roll and shoved it in her mouth.

"I expect to be back in time to wash up for the evening meal."

"That is good to hear," Selrach said, with a nod of his head.

"How so?"

"My bride enjoyed our short ride yesterday and had hoped to go riding again before the weather turned cold enough to provide more snowfall."

"You don't expect her to ride with us while checking for Raiders, do you?"

"I trust they are not so foolish as to still be around. Besides, you will have half the guard with you. I trust you will bring her back safely as you always have."

"Granted, I have been blessed with fortune when she has had need of me, but one day it will run out."

"Not so soon it will not, she has yet to give me children." Selrach flinched, 'Oops. I ought not to have said that.'

'What kids could Jannine want to talk to me about. Surely my brother... Parish the thought. What could it be?' He shook his head and laughed at himself for the thought. "I don't like it brother, but something tells me you will insist."

"See how well he knows me; he can even predict my mood," Selrach said with a smile towards his bride who now say chewing a sweet roll.

"I suppose we don't have to check all the caves in one day. We could even supervise the patrols from the Cliffs."

"Oh that would be lovely," said Jannine

'Lovely, that is not quite how I would put it.' "Well, I'm off to get the horses, I'll come for you when we are ready."

He got up and left with a determined stride, slamming the door behind him.

"That could have been more subtle," mother said. "I suppose you will want to sit with me when I meet with the Elders then, won't you Selrach."

"Believe it or not, their words carry a heavy weight on my mind. I would know what they think on this matter."

"And exactly what matter could it be that I am being left out of?" Rewdan asked, fascinated with the whole situation.

"I wish for Cirtap to accept Dan when we journey in the spring," said Jannine.

"That is a lot that you ask, I think it best if I join the guard today. With Cirtap's temper, Jannine may take courage in me as she tries to find her words," said Rewdan.

"Than I will join as well," said Garth. "And you can explain Dan to me."

"Thank you brothers. Cirtap had a point earlier and I am grateful for the extra men."

"We had better hurry up then. He won't wait for us in the mood he is already in," Rewdan said as he urged Garth towards the door.

"My child, you must take a second cloak with you today as the foam at the sea will add a chill to the air, then my maid can get you some heartier boots. Up with you, he may try to leave without you as well if he can," said mother.

No sooner had she stepped out the door wearing more clothes than she could carry, then Cirtap brought her mare to the door. "Your saddle awaits, my lady," he said.

Selrach took the honors and lifted her onto her seat.

"My love, will you help me with my skirts, it will be a long ride and I do not wish them to be soiled should I fall."

Selrach shook his head for forgetting how well she rode like a man, and walked around the outer side to lift her up again. She easily kicked her leg free, then he pulled the skirts down the back and sides of the horse. With the two cloaks and all the gowns, the horse would not be running much today. 'If this horse was not the one she had picked, and earned, I would insist she ride my large stallion, but he may be too much horse flesh for her to handle.' "Have a peaceful ride my sweet. I look forward to an early return," he gave her a kiss as she was just at his height and they were off.

Cirtap took the lead followed by Primo, then Rewdan and Garth. Jannine got to ride behind them, flanked by several of the guard. Cirtap would take no chances today. The rest of the guard followed at their leisure chatting amongst themselves, grateful for the chance to ride as he led them directly to the nearest cliff, then waited for them to gather.

"All right men, this should be a good day for a hard ride, I expect all of you to fill your lungs with sea air and get a good sweat out of your horses. There are three caves yet to the west and two to the east, all of which I can see from here. I expect those of you with the swiftest horses to ride down to the beaches and inspect the entrances for any recent signs of activity. There is no need to go in or take any risks of any kind. I want word of what you see, be it flint or burnt wood. I will tolerate no foolishness among my guard. That understood, enjoy the wind in your face and the sun on your back, spring is not to come for a while."

"Yes sir," they shouted in unison. Then off they went, shouting bets as to who would get to what cave first.

When they were all gone, Jannine approached Cirtap speaking as sweetly and softly as her native tongue would allow. "Nice ploy."

"Ya think?"

"Could not have predicted you would set them all so free."

"How else was I supposed to get rid of them? I know you want to talk to me, so out with it. What child could you and my brother be speaking of before the sun would rise?"

"How blunt and direct of you. If only you had presumed wrong. You do not make it easy for me to bring this up gently."

"I am not a gentle man."

"Liar!"

"Says you!"

"My first memory is of your gentle strength."

"You caused me to be curious, and so I was patient."

"Than I would ask you to be curious about somebody else's future and be patient with him."

She was trying to smile at him... "Him who?"

"Dan..."

"The bastard child of a treacherous whore? You have got to be joking, is this what it is all about? Let me guess, you would have me claim him and raise him as my own. Ha!"

"I would."

He looked at her harshly and spat, "You're serious, aren't you."

"Have you ever known me not to be?"

"Even after what his mother did to you, you would still grant him the honor of my house?"

Rewdan and Garth only looked at each other, as if asking if they should step in.

"His mother is a person that has paid for what she did. Blossom is no longer a factor unless you grant her low rank bearing."

He just looked at her, trying with all his might to not be angry with his future Queen. She was not yet through with his ears and he knew if he did not hear her out now, he would never hear the end of it.

"Dan is nothing more than a child, who happens to carry your blood. He can not help how that came to be and no other man can hold such power of what kind of man he becomes, as the man from whom he received his blood. It is your choice Cirtap. You can abandon him and hear of his treachery when your beard is gray, or you can ride him like a stallion into man hood. Break him, train him, and give him purpose in your life. A child can be a blessing or a curse. For the sake of the family, I am asking you to make him welcomed and loved. You once spoke of him with such affection in your eyes. Remember what that felt like? The child has never harmed me, and with your guidance, he may grow to be as honorable and trustworthy a man as the one before me now. He is so young Cirtap. Give him the right path on which to learn. Please..."

"You would have me bring him with us when we journey in the spring?"

"The sooner he feels the security you provide, the better."

"And what of when I must leave for battle?"

"Until he is of age to wield a sword at your side, he shall remain with me and help to prepare glorious feasts to celebrate your victories."

"Selrach already agrees?"

"He believes it wise for the boy to grow where he can see what a good man fathered him."

"And what if he also betrays me?"

"Then Selrach will have his head."

"Does mother also think this wise?"

"She thinks it worthy of speaking with the council of Elders about."

"No wonder he did not join us. My big brother goes behind my back!"

"Don't look at us," said Garth "We did not know till you had left to get her horse."

He looked back at Jannine and then down the cliff. The first of his men were already coming back.

"Cirtap, I ask you to give the boy a chance. Does he not deserve one chance to prove that he can learn from your example?"

"How can I love him when I see his mother soaking wet on the beach heavy with my child and ready to die, every time I look in his eyes?"

"That I cannot help you with. I can only pray that someday you will find a worthy bride, a woman who can help you to see Dan through her eyes. A woman who glows with pride at his strength and prays to be so blessed as to give you more sons just like him."

"You truly believe such a thing is possible?"

"I do."

"Then for your sake, I may take him in and add him to my prayers."

"Cirtap, I think they found something..." said Garth said in Cliff Tongue, bring their attention back to the warriors searching the caves.

"Where?"

"Look at the rider by the farthest cave. He has dismounted."

"Damned fool! Take her back to the long house, NOW!"

Cirtap took off like the wind and got to the beach before half his men noticed him riding.

When he pulled his horse to a stop, he almost yelled at his man, but stopped shy when he saw her. What remained of Blossom's body had washed ashore. Only the ice had left meat on her bones. The dress would have been unrecognizable, if not for the seal of his Mother's Village upon its breast. Tiny sea creatures were eating away at what remained beneath while the tide had washed something else clean enough to sparkle in the sunlight. He knelt down and rolled over the corps (causing his man to loose his breakfast) and revealed his brother's sword. 'She must have stolen it back and jumped overboard. Did she think this would redeem her? Did she have so little faith in the prophecy? Did she perhaps think the sword more valuable than Jannine?' However it came to be, his mother's blood had returned to its land.

"Get some more men and bury her under some rocks. I want no sign of her left on the beach. Report to me when it is done, my mother will want to see this immediately."

"Yes Sir."

Cirtap broke the sword free and slipped it into his belt before mounting.

He did not look back. The sight was already burned into his mind. He kicked his horse and took off into the forest at a canter. He was in no rush to walk in on their meeting, and he knew that his swift mount would get him there more than soon enough.

The sun was not yet fully high when Jannine, Rewdan, and Garth walked into the meeting at the Long House.

"Well, what did he say?" shouted Selrach.

"We were interrupted by a sighting on the beach, but I think I convinced him to give the child a chance. He has difficulty seeing Dan as his but instead only Blossom's. Under the current circumstances, that makes it worse. He said he would pray to be able to see the boy in a better light."

"Jannine, you work miracles. That is more than I had hoped for," said Selrach.

"I think that will conclude our meeting then," said one of the Elders, as he gestured the rest to leave.

"You give me too much credit, Selrach. I only begged him to open his heart," said Jannine.

"Begging had nothing to do with it," said Garth.

"You would have been proud to see her at him, both of you. He knew you had set him up and was just waiting to see what would make him angry. When she spoke the child's name, I saw the rage all but burst from his veins. The whole while, she never faltered. She pled her case as if scolding a child. She pounded sense and reason into him by forcing his own honorable deeds down his throat, saying that it was his choice to teach his son what kind of man to become," said Rewdan.

"And it worked," said Garth. "He was all but ready to apologize for not taking the child in sooner when I noticed one of his men dismounting on the beach."

"What did he find?" Asked Selrach.

"I don't know, Cirtap yelled at us to bring her back as he rode to see for himself," answered Rewdan.

"Mother what do you see?" Selrach asked.

The Queen stepped out onto the entry and stared into the sky, taking slow deep breaths as her children gathered around her....

"The woman has been granted forgiveness. Cirtap now has something new to be purified! The child will be made welcome, for Cirtap now has a new vision of the woman once known as Blossom."

Within a few moments, Cirtap's steed emerged from the trees. He gave the reins to a stable boy then approached the waiting gathering.

"I believe you have something for my daughter," said the Queen mother.

"Your sight grows strong! It would appear that Blossom was not a worthy offering to the sea as she stole this and jumped overboard too early," he pulled his brother's sword from his belt and placed it at his mother feet. "I believe you shall want to purify it before I return it to its rightful owner."

"That I will, immediately. Have the men build a fire within the Gathering. The flames shall carry all that remains of them far away," said the Queen.

Cirtap sent for the rest of the soldiers and a fire was built that would burn for several days. When it was ready to be lit, he called for his son.

"Dan, I have found forgiveness for your mother today. Her spirit bids me to claim you before all. So, I want you to take this sword in your hand... as it was the last thing your mother held," he picked up the child and helped him to bear the heavy weight then spoke to the people of the village. "Today, my son shall miss his mother no more. We grant her offering to the sun and stars and ask that it be purified. May this sword be as worthy of our future Queen's hand, as this child is of mine," he then turned and they placed the sword on the wood. With a torch, they set it aflame.

That night, Dan slept in the house of the Queen, as he did every night there after. The child was built a small box, which was placed against the wall by his father's chamber door. At night, Cirtap would leave the door open and they would hold hands till the boy went to sleep.

New life blew into Cirtap as he watched the flames. Day after day the fire raged. On the fourth day, a heavy snow came that snuffed out the last of the flames. The sword was retrieved from the ashes and Jannine spent several days polishing it till it shone anew.

On the day she felt it worthy of presenting to the people, a messenger came. The sword of the High King was complete. Jannine only smiled when the Queen presented it to her son.

"Mother, what do you speak of, I have a sword. My bride cleans it by my side and shall return it to me in finer condition than when I granted it to her," Selrach would enjoy this.

"No she will not. A Queen deserves a sword of her own. To her you gave it, and there it shall stay. Besides, it is by her sacrifices that you are able to receive such a sword. Only that which is forged of metal pulled from the boiling mud and cooled in the healing water, that she gathered, shall be worthy of a the High King. No Man shall stand against you as you wield this sword, and only thus shall you be able to rule all," the Queen declared.

"Oh, it is a fine sword indeed. But does it carry my blood? Does it carry that of my bride? Perhaps even my seed? It is a fine sword, mother, as any man can see, but what shall bond it to me? If only there was something to remind me...," he took the sword in his hands and gripped it firmly. "Oh yes, now I remember, the man gathering water did say something about a leather grip!"

Jannine burst out laughing at that, causing the Queen to stare at her.

"Look here brothers, how the leather has been bleached to be so soft and pale as my bride. If I did not know better, I would think she had helped with making even the leather grip!"

"Selrach please, if for nothing but my own dignity!"

"Oh my sweet," he makes a sniffing sound, "I can still smell my seed!"

"Selrach, you really are rotten, you know that!"

"You mean to tell me...," shouted the Queen.

All the men began to roar with laughter at the spectacle unfolding before them.

"That I have known of your gift since I took Jannine to the Lovers Pool? And Ooh how bad I have waited for this?" He gave the sword a swing with glee in his eyes, never had he received such a fine gift.

But his fun was not yet over... "And Ooh how I wish you could have seen it. There we were, totally nude and resting in the Lovers Pool, after quite an event! When this stump of a man so old and blind as to not see the torches, for the sunlight hurt his eyes, came walking right in on us! If I had had my sword I would have chopped his head off right then and there. Instead, my humble bride walks up to him, not even half covered and talks to him so sweetly that he trusts her as 'the honored guest of the Queen' and tells her of my mother's plan. And it gets better yet. My bride still full of that which I planted within, takes the bucket from the blind man, fills it partly with water from the pool, then sits upon it and fills it the remainder of the way. He then leaves vowing to have the leather placed upon the completed sword so that she may see it by this very full moon! You should have seen the look on his face when I said that I would be all too happy to hold my sword just as soon as he had it done!"

"Ooh brother, how did you keep such a tale for so long...," shouted Rewdan.

"Ooh, only for that very look on our dear mother's face!" he fell over laughing, and Jannine did not even try to hide her red face. "I had planned to send him a fine fur as thanks, but now I will have to send him two. Oh Mother, please forgive me, but for just once in my life, it felt good to know something that you did not! Ah ha ha ha"

"Dear son, how could I not forgive you? In fact, if I still walk the earth on your fiftieth winter, you may laugh as this once again. In the mean time, I have a feast to prepare."

She left them in her Long House to go find her Head Woman (any excuse to get out of there), he had earned the good laugh, but she did not have to stand there listening.

That night was a simple feast. Roots and meat had been cooked within the earth, then chopped and placed on several platters. Bread was broken and placed within baskets. As the snow had been falling steadily and the wind now began to rage, leather was placed over each dish and carried to the separate houses. Selrach personally delivered to each house as much as the occupants would need, and let all within admire his new sword before he went back to his Mother's Long House for the next house's load. When he finally returned, Jannine was waiting for him. All of the others had already gone to bed except the child Dan. He lay sleeping in her arms as she sat feeding the fire.

"One day, I shall walk through the door, and find you sitting so with my child in your arms," he said.

"I look forward to it," she replied.

"Do you really think this child will have a good future?" he asked.

"I dreamt of him last night teaching our son to fight. He carried his father's sword while our child carried yours. This is how I knew to have my sword done today. The sword our child carried was far too heavy, and Dan had to keep reminding him how to grip it and how to stand so that it would not pull him over."

"How old would you say they were?"

"Dan looked to be twelve while our son Selmore looked to be eight."

"Selmore?"

"Should your first born not be named after you?"

"Indeed he should. I was just surprised at the depth of your dreams."

"There is one thing that I do not understand."

"What is that?"

"The place they were playing in was nothing like this place. It was on the earth, yet had a solid wall around it."

"That is not so strange; your father's home is in the earth and has nothing but solid walls that arch into the ceiling."

"This place had no ceiling. Grass grew beneath their feet and the sun shown down on their heads yet early in the day."

"Perhaps this is a place still yet to be. The home that you grew in stands no more. I plan to build anew for you on that very sight. Perhaps the ashes will feed the grass."

"Perhaps..."

"Would you like me to put him to bed?"

"No thank you my love, I would like to hold him a bit longer. I am not yet ready for sleep and it gives me comfort to hold him. It is as if he teaches my body that this is what I should do. I pray that if I hold him enough, the moon will see me worthy of being a mother and grant me the child of my dreams."

"Then I will go to bed and dream of such sweet dreams," Selrach said before he laid a kiss on her cheek and went to bed.

That night by the fire, Evelyn guided Jannine with her first farsight through the flame...

She saw a girl, of no more that fourteen years, wearing a long white veil. She looked like a spirit, until she sat by the fire and removed the cloth revealing her pure body. Nothing was about her but the sticks and twigs that made her tiny hut. The girl lay down and pulled the cloth over her like a blanket, then cried herself to sleep. She prayed in a foreign Tongue before being replaced by another voice.

Somewhere else, another woman had lit a candle and said a prayer.

She had hair black as the night sky and skin tanned by the sun. She hid within a cave and the light of the candle glowed off the crystal walls. Jannine swayed to the rhythm of their beating hearts and asked to understand their prayers...

"Please let me be worthy..." called the girl.

"Please let him be honorable and trustworthy... " called the woman.

She thought of Rewdan and Cirtap, and sent their faces to the women...

"Be patient, he will come for you..."

Chapter Sixteen
The Horse Man

When the last of the snow finally melted on the ground surrounding the village, a rider arrived from the Plains bearing word from the King.

"King Kerill sends word to his new son. He is greatly pleased at word of his daughter's successful union and looks forward to her return. He plans to meet you in the village of her birth during the planting moon festival," said the rider.

"Mother, that leaves only ten days before us," exclaimed Selrach.

"My good man, you are welcome to travel home with our fleet as my sons will be leaving in only a few days," was the Queen's translation through Cirtap.

"Dear Queen, I thank you for the offer, but my King has already bid me to return with only one days rest. He sends me to escort the royal horses onto his land," said the rider.

"Your King is very generous as to send a guide and I am sure you will find the most lush feeding grounds, however I will not load a guest with such a burden to bear alone. As my sons will be sending many horses across the river, I will send five of my men to assist in your task," came another translation.

"That is not necessary, I am a master herder, as the young bride can verify."

"I wish that were true young man. However, the circumstances that brought me to these shores, with air still within my chest, cost me all of my memories. Your face is as familiar to me as fish within the sea," said Jannine.

"That is woeful indeed, for I remember well your dislike for their smell, let alone their taste," said the rider.

"Come over here my good man. Sit by your Prince and tell us of my sisters' lost memories," said Garth. "We shall fill your belly while you fill her mind."

"I would enjoy that my Lord," he said.

"Before you begin your tale, I must know your name," said Jannine.

"My name is Will, I served as stable boy on the farm at which you were raised. It was I who found you my Lord and drew you to her father's house," he said to Selrach. "It is heartening to see how well you both have fared since that terrible day."

"What all did happen? All we have is tiny pieces of dreams," said Selrach.

"When Jannine came of age during her fourteenth spring, word was sent to the King. He then sent forth one man of some weight within his guard to check on his child. Before the man left, he bade me to watch over her with the stealth that only a friend could provide. As we were already fast friends, it was little for me to include his demands within my daily tasks. On the day of the attack, I rose with the sun as I always did, to see Jannine just heading out for morning berries. I dressed and followed at my leisurely pace, always staying just around the bend. When she reached the trees near the jetty, she stopped and found something in the bushes. Before she left, she put her mother's cloak down, then ran back up the road holding something heavy to the other side of her body. I ducked behind a bush, as she was not to know that I followed, and let her run by. Once she had passed the next bend, I ran to your side and realized she would need help getting a wagon. I then turned to run, just as I heard her screaming."

"I took off like the wind, but I only caught up in time to see her being dragged aboard a rowboat. I knew immediately that I could no longer catch them, for it heaved in the river, caught by the outgoing tide. More men in the river called ashore, and I realized the farm was in danger. I then ran to the barn and caught two men fighting with her mare. I whistled and she bucked, knocking them both into the cellar. There I locked them in, and there they died, as I released all the horses and hooked up a wagon to her mare. Before I left, I saw Raiders leaving the house and setting it ablaze, they yelled something at the barn, so I ran out the back, knocking over a couple lanterns in my wake. The straw quickly fed the blaze and I saw the Raiders laughing when they turned toward their ship, which had docked beyond a heavy thicket of trees. I got you sir and took you straight to the King," said Will.

"Why did you not come to the village?" asked Rewdan.

"I was not sure how many of the Raiders might have come ashore as Traders, and I also knew it would take two days, walking through the night, to reach the King's farm. It was the only place I knew this strange man would be truly safe, and they could also provide the best medicine for him there. Many a warrior has been healed within the Queen's home. Besides, any man who would receive the Princesses' cloak, must be judged worthy by the King," said Will.

"If only we had met on the road," said Rewdan. "We searched for days."

"Actually, Sir, I think we did. Was it not you who rode with seven men on stallions past me yet early in the first day and then again late into that night? You asked me if I knew of the King's dwelling. I said that all the Plains People know to seek their King within the Earth. You asked me where in the Earth. And I answered, 'where he found his bride.' All the Plains People know that they first met when she had walked for three days south from the Pool of Deep Water. He found her near death from dehydration in the High Dessert and dug a well to nourish her. That is where they built their home and that is where she conceived his two sons. We were at the point in the road marked for the fourth day of walking south from the Pool of Deep Water. Do you remember the stones?" asked Will.

"Do you mean the boulders?" Asked Rewdan.

"They were put in place so that all his people could find their King within the first year of their union," said Will. "Similar markers lay across our entire land. They point the way and count the days. Any person who seeks his council or judgment may seek him out by simply following the stones! 'As the Holly water feeds our land from below. Stones of hope skip across its surface'!"

"I've heard that before, and for now of all times for me to finally know what it means. Dear brother, you call me a linguist and yet my ignorance of the culture failed you," said Rewdan.

"Sir, it was always meant as a ruse. It is a matter of safety for the King! Only do invited guests know how or where to find him. Even his people do not know when he will be at home. On my life, I could not explain further at the time," said Will.

"But I passed you twice, and saw nothing but branches in your wagon!"

"What better to hide him under that which my lady had found him!"

"The King was wise to put his faith in you," was Cirtap's translation from the Queen. "You are truly wise and loyal. But what of my son's bride, I wish to hear tales of her youth."

"Yes dear Queen, My favorite memory is that of the spring festival. Not but this last year did Jannine compete. It was the first year her father had granted permission that she been seen in a public gathering. Though her name could be known, her origins were forbidden to be revealed. Knowing such, I was sent to accompany her to a spring festival three hard days ride to the east where she might compete without her face being recognized. Her father had granted her admission into only one game, so she chose the hunt."

"We have a game by that name; she is a devious master indeed!" Cirtap said with a laugh.

"On the Plains, the competition is three days. Normally it is reserved for men, and only the finest hunters compete. Since Jannine, they have had to open it up for those women who can afford to compete. The first task consists of seven horses having large sacks of straw strapped on their backs. Blood is poured on the surface to make a mark visible to all. Then they are set loose in a wide-open field. The competitor must then mount their own horse and ride into the field. He that hits the targets best without harming the horses, wins. For Jannine, they set only four horses loose. When she had shot them all, she returned to the last three still tied to a tree and shot them as well. Then she shouted that 'the judges must think women only hunt sick game!' She was ranked eighth out of twenty-seven, and moved on to the next round."

After a pause, Will continued, "On the second day, those who compete in the hunt must race each other through an obstacle course collecting cloth from trees. Jannine easily returned first by grabbing the lowest cloth on each tree while the men fought over the ones within reach of their mighty stallions. On the third day, the hunters must ride a canoe down a river. He who survives with the most fish wins the day, and possibly high honors! Jannine had no desire to win the day, or high honors, so she told me to meet her back at the end of the course. She guided through the rapids easily enough and took a nap through the shallows. When she approached the final bend, she tipped the canoe over and let it float belly up to the finishing beach. I met her around the next bend with a dry vest and her mother's cloak. She had no desire to be around when honors were handed out, so we left for home once she had changed and dried."

"Wait a minute, changed? Into what?" asked Cirtap.

"Her leggings and vest."

"Leggings... and vest?" questioned Rewdan.

"Yes Sir. Why? She always dressed like that on horseback. She told me once that as best friends, she never wanted me to see her as a girl, besides men would not see her as desirable if she did not have skirts they could lift! She hated dressing for the old ladies. I always new it would be a bad day when I saw her emerge before the sun, bound as a Pure and Humble Maiden. She knew that if men thought they could not have her, that they would want her even more. This would not be good for if any threat should reach her father's ears, then she would no longer be granted the freedom to ride! Unfortunately, the women of the village held a council and decided she should have more modesty forced on her early in the spring of her fifteenth year. After that, she had to spend four days a phase spending from mid day to setting sun, quietly serving drink to the Traders. After an incident where she poured a jug of wine over a Trader's head, she was forced to add tending flowers from sun up till mid day two of those days every phase. Even if she should have been sequestered."

"Secweahh?" asked Rewdan

"It is when a woman must be alone during the fourth phase!"

"We have a women's house for that!" said Jannine.

"Every time they made her tend the Traders during those times, something always happened!"

"Like what?" asked Selrach.

"Men could be served meat not yet cooked or fruit with worms in them. I even heard of her kicking a man between the legs so hard that he bled for a week."

"What had he done?" asked Cirtap

"He got drunk and grabbed her by the skirt, and then he tried to kiss her!"

"You should count yourself lucky brother!" Rewdan said to Cirtap.

"What ever for?" asked Will.

"After he returned with her from the River of Life, he took her Gift of Tongue as a reward for his services rendered! Then she slapped him so hard as to leave a mark that would last for three days!" said Rewdan.

"And if you hadn't been second, she would have gotten you too for setting up the little joke!" said Cirtap.

"I still think he deserves it," said Jannine.

"What, you said you forgave me," he pleaded.

"That has nothing to do with whether or not you deserved it, only whether you got it!" she said.

"Well put my bride!"

"I can see her spirit has not changed as her appearance has," said Will.

"Other than her fine gown, how has she changed?" asked Selrach.

"She now is all too happy to sit closely by your side with your hand upon her thigh! And she not only has her hair up and back, but also bound. Before, she used to restrain her hair from the wind blowing it in her face! Now she has it more tightly bound when sheltered from the wind! Also, though she is much thinner than she would have been while riding on the Plains, there is a glow in her face that I have never seen before. It is as if her face can not help but smile."

"She has looked that way ever since she emerged on the second day after being bonded. We presented her with the dress she now wears along with several others and she insisted on hosting several nights of feasting to thank this village for making them," said Cirtap.

"Now thanking the village sounds like Jannine, but why the dresses?"

"She had saved all that she had for me," replied Selrach. "On our first night she gave me all that she had and was very upset when emerging on our first day, in such a horrible way that all our brothers saw her full beauty. She no longer wants any man to ever see the flesh that she has given me. It was actually rather quite genius of my brothers to find this fabric and have such lovely gowns cut for her."

"But what will she wear upon her return to the Plains?" asked Will.

"What do you mean?" asked Jannine.

"The summer weather is much too hot and sticky for such fabrics. And the grasses will catch in your skirts."

"Dear Selrach, I do believe he offers me a challenge."

"I will look forward to your resolution upon returning from my first trip," Selrach said as he kissed her lips.

"Well, if you don't mind old friend, you have shocked me enough for one night. I should now ask where I bed," said Will.

"I'll show you, there is room enough in Primo's house, and we can speak of my father before we sleep," said Garth.

"Well then," Will said as he stood, and reached out both hands to Jannine.

Jannine looked at him funny, stood, and rose both hands to him. He grasped both hands so that their palms touched as they stood at arms length from each other. He then put a leg behind his other and ever so barely bowed. She tried to copy before he let go and walked out the door.

"For as wonderful as it is to hear the joy in his voice telling such stories, it is disheartening to not know how to say goodnight," Jannine said in cliff tongue as the men left.

"Now that I can explain," said Rewdan. "That is how blood-brothers say farewell. Sometime in your past, one of you must have saved the life of the other. Only when blood is shed can hands be bonded. Once united, the blood bond swears allegiance to your dying day. As Cliff Dwellers kiss on the cheek to show they care, Plainsmen forge hands to build a bridge across the river granting life to a friend. It is a sign of respect as well as affection," said Rewdan.

"I can't help but wonder how much of his mind is filled with my memories..."

"Not as many as there will be when he dies. As your stable boy, and now herder, the King has granted him a lifetime of servitude to you. He will never leave your side unless you go to sea."

"Selrach, I wish to sleep now. My mind needs time to put these new memories away."

"I will kiss you later then, and speak of packing horses with my brothers for a while."

"Yes my love," said Jannine.

She left the men and crawled into bed, pondering the thought of wearing a vest and leggings while riding across a never-ending field.

When Jannine woke in the morning, she dressed herself quickly and emerged to find that all her brothers had already fed and gone with her man to pack the horses. She immediately shoved a roll in her mouth and ran out to the porch to see for herself the excitement. Twenty war horses had been brought into the gathering and were being set with packs as Jannine ran to the house where Mother's head woman lived.

"Please tell me you have them ready," Jannine shouted when she burst through the door.

"I finished them last night when I heard of the rider's arrival," said the woman.

"May I be granted a Head Woman as wonderful as you," Jannine shouted, hugging the woman about the neck. "May I see them?"

"Right here my Lady," she said.

Jannine looked at the leather pouches beside the fire and unfolded the first one. Within, she found a cloth three times longer than she was tall. All the edges were trimmed with fine embroidery that could only be compared to that in her own gown. When she held it in the light, it shimmered like the morning fog and when folded on a pile, it had a sheen of pale green. "Such cloth will bind her beautifully," said Jannine, replacing the fabric within its leather pouch.

"May I ask who, my Lady?" Said the woman.

"Rewdan's bride. She waits for him in the Land of Mist. And this one is for Cirtap's bride who hides on an Island."

She opened up the package to find cream colored cloth as smooth as coconut milk. Several strips of cloth had been sewn to overlap one another creating a layered effect that would hang from the neck and only allow that which hung about her feet to float on the breeze.

"These will be my gift to welcome them into my family," Jannine said.

"Never have I seen such gowns, My Lady. How did you know how to have them cut?"

"I have been visiting them every night in my dreams. Ever since the first time I saw them by light of the fire. Oh, and you must remain to your oath of secrecy; Rewdan and Cirtap do not yet know their brides await them."

"As you wish, my lady."

Jannine then took the two packages and returned to the Queen's Long House. Once there, she was all too grateful to find her alone. "Mother, I have something for you to study, and it must be quick."

"What ever could you be shoving under my sight?" the Queen said as they were laid on her lap.

"For nearly two moons, I have had your Head Woman working on a most secret task, and now I ask for your blessing. On the night that my man granted feast to the village who admired his sword, I sat by firelight holding my brother's son. That night the fire granted me sight of two worthy brides. I prayed to my mother and was granted a glimpse of their thoughts. A girl of the Mist prayed to be worthy of a foreign prince and a woman of the Islands prayed for a warrior that was honorable and trustworthy. I have been sending them the sight of my brothers every night in my dreams. These dresses are to be the first gift they shall receive. I bring them to you now so that you will recognize them when you allow your sight to travel and see your sons. I want you to be able to see how well they fare more easily," concluded Jannine.

The Queen placed her hand within the first package, "This is for a child who worries much, she will need the passionate and confidant persuasion that only my Rewdan can provide. She will serve him well so long as he is patiently firm."

She then placed a hand into the second package, "This woman's path of vengeance leads her into our circle of loyalty. She is strong willed and determined. She will be a fine match to Cirtaps' temper."

She handed the packages back to Jannine. "You have chosen well. Should your dreams come to pass as mine have, you will have a strong group bound to your table. I will do all that I can to help them by day. While you however, must mix words to make my sons hurry across the sea before the Sea King knows of your task."

"With all the haste your breath can muster, mother."

"Then you must make haste, the men have decided to send the horses yet this very day."

"Then I must find Primo. He is the only one I trust with the task of delivering them. Rewdan will only take his bride when forced to, after seeking her Tongue as the people of the Mist are much more conservative with their princess than I."

Out she ran and found Primo already mounted as he had offered to join the herding party.

She found her horse near the entry and mounted to ride with him down to the first river where they would split and make camp for the ships.

"Primo, I must speak with you," she called in her native tongue, hoping to not draw attention.

"Yes my Lady, anything I can help you with?" said Primo.

They were at a place within the line, that they were surrounded by horses, allowing them privacy to speak freely.

"I have a task for you of some discretion," she said at last.

"I am intrigued. Just what all does this task entail?"

"I have two gifts within these packages. You must keep them with you at all times. I grant you the task of keeping them safe and dry, as the fabric contained within is as precious and fine, as to grant my brother's salvation. You will stand by their sides, wherever they may journey this coming year, once they leave the festival and keep these with you always. When Rewdan takes the Tongue from a girl of the Land of Mist, this package will save a life." She hands him the first one. She then passed him the second one as she says, "Cirtap will need this before his voyage to the Islands comes to an end."

She pulled her horse to a stop and he pulled out of rank to stay at her side. "This is of the utmost importance Primo. Do not speak to anyone of these packages, especially my brothers. They must find their own paths if these gifts are to be granted to one who is truly worthy."

"I understand my Lady. My lips will not open unless commanded," said Primo.

"Should my brothers suspect anything and push demands on you, tell them I bade you carry forth these gifts and swore you to silence on the cost of your head. They will not question you further and respect my decision, though my man may be persuaded to ask again. When he does, speak with him alone and tell him that I only wish for his brothers to find a blessing such as his. He alone may see the contents before they are delivered."

"Yes my lady. I will stand firm to your word even should Cirtap draw on me."

"I pray that he be not so rash for I hope to entrust you with many a task before you are laid within the earth."

"I look forward to it, and hope I shall be granted as good a laugh as your man for holding my Tongue so tight."

"If my dreams come to pass, we all will. In the mean time, I was also hoping for a word with Will before you take his lead. You would not be so wise as to know where I might find him, would you?"

"He has already taken the lead with your man. He has been filling Selrach's ears all morning," said Primo.

"Then I believe I shall feel the wind in my hair today," the future Queen said, giving her mare a spur in the side.

She had a glorious ride finding the head of the chain before kissing her man when she arrived.

"Shall I not share in the stories today?" she asked.

"But my sweet, it is because you shared in the stories that we have them to hear," replied her future King.

"And just what exactly has this man told you while I was not present?" she asked.

"That when your foster mother was with child during a harsh winter, you both became so ill from all the fish and lobster brought in by the hunters at sea, that you taught yourself to hunt rabbit with your bow. Then you spent every day seeking tracks in the snow just so that you would not have to suffer eating meat off the sea," Selrach said as the other men laughed.

"Well then my Love, I look forward to testing my skills once again, only perhaps now I will seek more substantial prey," she shot a piercing look past him that made his brothers go quiet. "What I am currently hoping for is a chance to speak with our guest before he strides across the land."

"Then I will grant you the lead my sweet," he said as he faded back.

"I have been hoping to learn how it comes to pass that you and I are bonded by blood," she told Will.

"Deep inside you already know, otherwise you would not have asked that we speak alone."

"Please, help put it back into my mind."

"As you wish. One hot summer day, when I was in my fourteenth summer and you were in your twelfth, we went swimming in the river. We were still young enough to disrobe before entering the cool water and had enjoyed the river so on many occasions. On this day, we had not accurately predicted the tide and were overcome by the rising sea. You took a deep breath and went under near the middle of the river while I fought the waves near shore. When the worst had passed, you came up cleanly only to see me loose the fight. I went under and you found me unconscious after being washed against the rocks. You pulled me up and onto the shore. Than you held the blood within my hair as I struggled to get air back into my chest. That day was the last time I ever entered the water for sport, and you vowed to never swim near the ocean again. I regained my feet and we walked back to the barn as you were called to dinner. When you turned to leave, we saw that you still had blood on your hands. In a panic, you went to wash it in the horses' trough... and when I dipped my hands in to help, we clasped hands, vowing to never let the other come so close to death again. It then became tradition for us to say good night, as we did last night, every night in the barn before you went in for the evening meal. So it has been for the last five years."

"And so it shall continue to be. I am eternally grateful to you for saving my man and my memories. And Will, I look forward to you helping me build my home."

"Pardon?"

"My man intends to rebuild in the place of my birth."

"Such a place is unsafe. It lays on the outermost edges of our land, and the Raiders grow more desperate."

"Then we will have to build a house the likes of which they can neither enter or burn down," Jannine said.

"The likes of which I have never seen," said Will.

"And thus all who are granted passage within will know it is the house of the High King!"

"You have always insisted on being unique! I have no doubt that your house will be as well," confirmed Will.

They arrived at the sight of the riverside camp a short time later, to see the river already swelling up on the rocky banks.

"The river is already beginning to rise as I had feared," he said.

Jannine could see the concern in his eyes and reached for Will's hands while they were still mounted. "Then I will wish you a swift and safe journey," said Jannine.

Under the best conditions, it would take them nearly two phases to bring the herd to her village, so she quickly dismounted and handed him the reins with a smile. Half the men also dismounted and tied their horses in the longest chain they had ever seen. Will took the lead and went to where the river ran it's widest so that the horses would cross in the rocky shallows.

From then on, Jannine could do nothing but stand on the shore and watch as the last of them disappeared over the far ridge. When she finally turned around, the men had already spread out the tarps that would make up the Great Tent. Tonight it would actually be half full. Selrach, Rewdan, Cirtap, Garth and Jannine would all bed down early, as would many of their men, for the following day would bring a long day of working on the ships in hopes that the river did not rise too quickly.

Chapter Seventeen
Making Waves

Cirtap was the first to rise, followed by Garth. They emerged from the tent early enough that the sun had not yet broken the horizon, as Cirtap rubbed his hands together before grabbing more wood for the fire.

"Will you be quiet? You will wake the others, and my sister hates the cold mornings," said Garth.

"I know, but she has my brother to keep her warm now, so I don't expect them to get up for a while. In fact, if I know Selrach, he will thank me later for getting Rewdan out of the tent! Besides, my men slept early last night so that we could beat the sun. The warmer it gets, the more the snow will melt, and we need all the time we can steal from the sun if these ships are to be sea worthy before the first mountain tides," defended Cirtap.

"I know, I just wish I was still in bed with a warm woman beside me."

"You will make a terrible Warrior."

"Come here now, you can't tell me that you don't count the days till that is you in there ignoring the sun."

"I do not."

"Liar"

"How dare you. If I was not use to such treacherous words from your sister..."

"You'll what, admit that it is nice to have a good woman about camp."

"It is good and bad at the same time. My men will be distracted."

"You are distracted. Your men take heart in her as she has already become a symbol of hope. Every time they look at her, they see a future worth fighting for, like nothing before. I've seen it, and so have you," said Garth.

"Yes I have, and that is what worries me. What if something were to happen? Every last one of them would drop what they are doing to come to her side."

"Than it will be your job to remind them of where they are needed. For a Warrior, you have a gift with words. When the time comes, I have no doubt that the Captain will lead his men well," said Garth.

"For a foreigner, you sure do seem confident," said Cirtap.

"Soon, it will be you who is the foreigner. Yet we will still be brothers. I'm sorry for calling you what I did, but you should learn, there is nothing you can hide from a child of the earth. Not even the deepest secrets of your heart," said Garth.

"And what do you know of secrets?" challenged Cirtap.

Garth sat by his side and leaned over as if to merely poor hot water in his morning tea while he whispered, "I know that you dream of a virgin bride that will be as affectionate, eager, and loyal, as the one your brother has."

He then sat back and sipped his own tea, while looking over the edge of his cup.

"That is not such a big secret, ask Rewdan... Many men are envious of my brother," said Cirtap.

"The others are more able to control their eyes," said a mumbled voice in a cup.

'Have I really been so careless? Can my new brother really be so insightful all on his own?' "And what do you say of the Captain of the guard supervising the future Queen's activities?" were the next words put forth by Cirtap.

"I would say that the Captain has already proven his loyalty and now needs to find a trustworthy man to delegate some of the responsibility too. I would hate for another missed opportunity to further cloud your vision."

"And exactly which opportunity are you thinking of..."

"I was watching, as my mother had taught me, the night you fought with Blossom in the snow. I saw the look in your eyes when you embraced my sister. I know where your heart lays Cirtap, and I'm telling you now. If you are to be ready for the woman who awaits you, you must let go of Jannine. Today, you must look on her no more. Today, you must assign her a new guard. One so unworthy that he would never look on her with hope."

Garth then got up and left to walk down the beach as the rising sun danced on the water.

Cirtap just sat there contemplating his words. 'Garth really is loyal to me. He is also right. I do want to move on to a woman of my own but whom, when, where? Is there really such a thing as hope in finding a second worthy bride? Mother has never spoken of such a prophecy... Perhaps mother has not told us all. It would not be the first time. Yet if Garth has seen me hoping for another kiss, than maybe he has also seen another. It is time I delegated more...'

He needed someone that he could leave behind when they left to trade. 'Primo recommended that Ron take his place by my side in his absence. He is a good Warrior who knows Clear River and is fluent in Plains Tongue.' Cirtap could not think of a single thing to cause him to doubt Ron would be a good choice. It was settled then. He would begin having Ron check in on her. 'She could easily grow to trust him as well as Primo.'

The thought heartened him. Now when they arrived in the land of the Plains People, she would have two trustworthy guards that would never leave her unattended. Will and Ron! Cirtap finished his tea and walked the camp, kicking the feet of his men that still dared to sleep now that the sun shone on his fire.

Jannine awoke to the sound of Cirtap grumbling at those still sleeping beyond. With a smile on her face, she quickly got up and dressed, then turned to wake her man and brother.

"Selrach my love, you must rise... Your brother awakens the men without you." She then turned and pushed her brother. "Rewdan, would you have your men think you lazy, or just too good to help."

"Oh woman, we shall rise in good time," grumbled Selrach.

"Your men do not have the luxury of such a tent to shield the sun from their eyes. Would you have them start the day without you?" she knew she was pushing, but they were not taking the lead as their brother had.

"My men will think that my bride has granted me a blessed morning before our journey," came Selrachs' defense.

"Not so my love. They know of my great discretion and would never think such a thing while your brother remains within," Jannine was smiling from ear to ear now. At least he would be up, and Rewdan would be forced to get out and do something.

"You are right my sweet, bachelors have little reason for lying beneath such a glorious sunrise. Up and out with you, you lazy fool. Your brother has shamed you with his vigilance," commanded Selrach.

"Do I at least get to eat first?"

"There is nothing for you to dine on within this tent. I shall enjoy my breakfast in peace," Selrach said as he shoved Rewdan out the door with his shirt and vest in his hands.

"And what exactly do you think you are going to have for breakfast?" asked Jannine.

"Only my favorite thing I like to eat," Selrach said, pushing her against the table.

"You are as foolish as your brother for looking at me so. What if your men should over hear?"

"Than I shall have to muffle your mouth with mine," he said while lifting her skirts.

"It is good to see you have decided to help," Cirtap declared.

"I did not decide anything, they decided for me," said Rewdan.

"Never the less, work you shall. I already have two groups of men working on pitching the boats. I want to have them turned yet today!"

declared Cirtap.

"Today? How hard do you plan to push them?"

"Hard enough to be early."

"But they will have nothing left in them but sleep," argued Rewdan.

"Good, There will be plenty time for sleeping once we make waves."

"You sound as bad as that woman of his. She seems to think me lazy."

"That makes too of us! Now get that roll in your mouth and pick up a shovel. We have trenches to dig," barked Cirtap.

Rewdan bent his back in spite that day, and for another two more, until all three ships were in the bay. On the third day, half the village arrived to see them off. The Queen brought fresh food stocks and Cirtap's son, Dan. When all were finally aboard, the Queen bade them farewell from the first rising cliff.

The food stores came in handy during their voyage as the cold wind blew hard at their back, making fishing unsuccessful. And as they were all eager to arrive in Jannines' village of the Plains People at the port of Clear River, Cirtap deemed it best to sail through the night. Those Warriors accustomed to sleeping on shore after hunting fresh game were told they could remain in the village and hunt the land of the Plains while the true Warriors gathered game afoot at sea. After five men had been told this on the eve of the first day, the rest of the trip went as smoothly as the wind on the water. Even the tides seemed to favor them, for they pulled into the third largest trading dock built by the Plains People on the morning of the fifth day.

Chapter Eighteen
Matchmaker

Everything seemed strange and new to Jannine, but Selrach made it his pleasure to point out certain buildings and land marks while people started waving and calling her name as if they knew her. When she finally set foot on the dock, no less than fifty people crowded around to see. Jannine looked up at her man. Fear was all he saw in her eyes...

"My sweet, these are your friends, your neighbors. They know you, love you, and miss you."

"But they know everything about me and I know nothing of them. They look as if they could hold me so tight as to take my breath, yet I don't know a single one of their names. How many of them would tell us falsehoods. How many would act like my friends only now that I am to be Queen. Selrach, neighbors they may be, but something tells me not to trust them."

"Hold my hand and you will be fine, I will only introduce you to those I know," Selrach said, hoping to reassure her.

"I may be able to help with that. That man holding the first line was your foster father at the farm. His bride is the woman in the tattered red dress just beyond the crowd," said Garth.

Rewdan and Cirtap followed, as did the rest of the men, and they slowly made their way to solid ground. Jannine held firm to the men of the Cliffs that she had known all winter, and they let only those locals through that the brothers recognized and called by name. Eventually most everybody got a hint and went back to their tasks as before. Cirtap gave some of his men orders to take the larger ship up along the coast and anchor it near the farm, while others were sent to begin unpacking the trade goods. Ron was then given a list of goods that were to be set aside within a hull as a gift to the King for granting his daughter into a blessed union. When Cirtap was satisfied that the men would be kept busy and out of trouble, the family headed to the Village House where they could be served cold drink and meat with select members of the community.

By evening time, Jannine's mind was racing from all the talk of Trade and Raiders and what future plans the Princes might have. So she left the discussions and went for a walk.

The main road to the dock had been filled with tables from every house in the village, and girls of all ages were talking while arranging for the coming feast. When the first girl saw her, she knew it was too late to turn back.

"Jannine!" squealed a girl of sixteen with long hair the color of wheat.

"Yes?"

"Come here. We are all dyeing to know what the Cliffmen are like. Is it true what they say?"

"It would help if you told me what they say."

"That the Cliff Dwelling men not only steal your Tongue, but they have a pool that causes women to steal their Tongue!"

Jannine could not help but smile, "It is true."

"Jannine, can you actually speak with them... YOU know in the Tongue of the Cliff Dwellers?" asked a girl the same age as her.

"I only just gained the Gift of Cliff Tongue from my man at the pool two moons past, but yes."

"You gained Full Tongue?" questioned a rather rude looking girl.

"Yes, I am now as fluent in their Tongue as I am in mine."

"But how did you ever become bonded?"

"I met my man here the morning the Raiders came. I gave him my Tongue then so that he might be able to survive."

"You mean you kissed an absolute stranger! Not you of all girls would ever do that! I don't believe you!" interrupted the rude one.

"I found him half dead on the side of the road, I can't remember anything else. I do know that my first memory is of his eyes."

"But where did you go?" asked a girl, little more than a child.

"I was taken by the Raiders and then rescued by my man's brother when the Raiders sought ground on their land."

"But how did they know to rescue you!"

"They did not. They found me tied up in the cargo hold after the battle."

"You mean they actually took a Raiders ship?"

"The large one sent along the coast is that very ship."

"Oh Jannine, such adventure!" cried a rather plump and sweet face. "You don't think we could be so fortunate?"

"I do indeed. However, you must be coy. They like a woman who can offer proof."

"Proof of what?" asked the rude one.

"Proof that you are a virgin when first taken as a bride."

"You're joking!" shouted the first girl.

"You can not imagine how embarrassed I was to wake on the first day, and my man had granted the Elders our Bridal Fur!"

"Oh Jannine!" they all cried.

"How did you ever get through it?" asked the girl with fair hair.

"I talked to my man and he explained how important it was and how much more they now respected me for it. Then we spent the whole day alone. When we got up the next morning, the village had made me a gift of thanks."

"What ever could be so great," said a stocky girl toward the back.

"They made me this gown and several others so that I would never have to let any but my man see anything of mine ever again!" Jannine replied with confidence.

"Dresses! They took your Decency and gave you Dresses! Not

much of a trade," she said.

"It is more than that, I gained their respect. They know heed my words as if I were their Queen."

"Jannine, Don't be so bold! One could only hope for such a thing. Besides, Selrach is handsome, but he is just a Trader," said the girl with fair hair.

"He trades his mother's goods."

"Even worse, he has no property of his own!" said the rude girl.

"His mother is Queen Jacqueline, Sorceress of the Wind and Ruler of the Cliff Dwellers," announced Jannine.

The rude girl looked as if she was about to swallow her tongue. "Does he know you use to serve wine in the Village House?" was the best she could come up with.

"That is where he first laid eyes on me. He later walked the coastal road to seek me out when the Raiders attacked him and left him for dead. In fact, I have since served wine and beer to every single one of his guests," Jannine was smiling with pride now.

"I suppose a good Queen should come from humble roots," said the plump girl.

"That is exactly why my man is so grateful to have me."

"You don't suppose that his brothers are looking in kind, do you?" asked the girl with fair hair.

This caught her off guard. 'Now what do I do? Think faster....' "They are looking indeed. However, they hope to out do their brother by finding women just as pure but of more exotic origins. They want their Kingdom to be known for Trading with all the lands. However, they do have several men who will be staying to watch over me when they leave who are yet to bond."

"Really?" said the plump one with an eager look on her face.

"Please tell me, what is your name?"

"You really have lost your memories haven't you Jannine. I'm Sarah!"

"Let's take a walk Sarah."

The rest of the girls stayed behind and watched Jannine lead Sarah to the two Trade Ships on the pier.

"Hello."

"Yes my Lady" came the voice of a young guard. Jannine recognized him immediately. He was an avid hunter who had been seasick and thus named one of the five to stay behind.

"Is your name not John?"

"It is my Lady, so good to know you remembered."

"I would like to introduce you to a friend of mine, her name is Sarah."

At the sound of her name she smiled and curtsied.

"Yes my lady. How may I help you?"

"Tell me, do you think her pretty?"

"My lady?"

"In all honesty, you must tell me."

"Why yes, my Lady, of course my Lady."

"Exactly why do you think her pretty?"

"My lady, I ought not speak of such things."

"Tell me now or you shall have to tell me before your lord."

He suddenly looked shocked and scared...

"It... is... just... that...."

"I command you to stop stuttering and spit it out."

"I like a young woman with bountiful breasts, My Lady!"

Jannine smiled at Sarah before asking, "How old are you?"

"I am entering my seventeenth summer."

"You have no woman either, correct?"

"That is correct my Lady. Why?"

"Sarah, thinks you are a very tall and handsome foreigner."

John smiled at Sarah and she smiled back.

"Sarah, I bet if you tried to take his Gift of Tongue, he would let you!"

"Jannine, you have got to be joking! Why I could never..."

"If you don't, you will never hear him say how much he is attracted to you. He is much to shy to take the Gift of Tongue from you!"

Jannine whispered before smiling and slowly walking away.

"My lady? Is there something I missed?"

"There is much you may miss, if you two don't get over being so shy!"

With that, she almost ran down the dock.

When she turned around, John stood staring into Sarah's eyes. Suddenly, Sarah jumped on him so hard as to knock him over with a smothering kiss. Jannine saw her skirts fly as they rolled over each other trying to be the one to take a bigger kiss. The girls on shore began screaming with glee causing the rest of the men to come up on deck. They started cooing when the couple finally stopped for air.

Cirtap, of course, came running at the commotion, followed by everybody that had been in on the discussion in the Village House and heard the shouting. Jannine just stood holding her hands at the foot of the dock, blocking their path, with absolute glee all over her face.

"What on earth is going on here?" Cirtap shouted at is Warriors.

John immediately came running down the pier and knelt before his Captain.

"Oh Cirtap, don't be angry. It was all my doing," said Jannine

"And exactly what is your doing?"

"My dear friend wished to be introduced to one of the handsome young guard you have designated to remain behind."

She was smiling from ear to ear, and could barely contain herself.

"I have never heard of an introduction causing such a ruckus," Cirtap replied, obviously still upset.

His anger frightened Sarah so much that she grabbed John's hand and tried to hide behind him.

"Exactly what is she looking at?" Cirtap said, with out thinking, in his own Tongue of the Cliffs.

"A very foul tempered brute of a man." Sarah said... in the Tongue of the Cliff Dwellers.

The gathered crowd suddenly went silent at the sound of her voice speaking a foreign Tongue.

"Now I understand," said Cirtap, in the Tongue of the Plains People.

"So you are not angry?" asked John... in the Tongue of the Plains People.

"Nope!"

"Really, Cirtap. You are not angry?" pleaded Jannine.

"Nope!"

"That's so wonderful to hear," Jannine said with a deep exhale. "I'm not angry at all. You want to know why?"

Now Cirtap was smiling and Jannine got suspicious...

"Why?"

Cirtap switched to Cliff Tongue before speaking loud and clear that his select audience would head every word. "Because you get to explain to her father why these two are getting bonded tonight!" He looked at Jannine, then John, and then the men standing on deck. "Remember this men, ALL gifts come at a sacrifice and I will not tolerate my men being greedy and disrespectful. Honor shall be the only thing to touch your lips unless you count yourselves home!"

Sarah gasped as John clutched her in his arms.

"I do believe the large man pushing his way through the crowd might just be her father coming now. Have fun cleaning up your mess little sister."

He strode past the man and quickly pulled his brothers back into the Village House as the crowd turned their attention to Jannine.

"Just what is going on here Sarah?" asked a man, half confused and half angry.

"I... Ah..., its' just that, well Jannine said..."

"If I may introduce myself, I am Princess Jannine, Pure Bride to Prince Selrach of the Cliff Dwellers and daughter of your King Kerill."

"No you're not! You're that girl Jannine that was taken by the Raiders last fall," he said, rather perturbed by her outrageous statement.

"My good man, I am one in the same and I Will NOT tolerate being interrupted again! My man plans to build a new Royal House on the land of which my mother died giving me life and which I was raised. Good Sarah has asked that she be granted the blessing of working as a Head Woman in my home. This Honorable Young Warrior who is to remain as my personal guard has just taken the Gift of her Tongue in hopes that it will lead to a happy union within my house. I expect that such a man as you would only count himself blessed to have such a fine daughter as to be instantly recognized as a truly faithful and loyal maiden of the Plains People. One so loyal that this good man is only too happy to take her as his most honored Pure Bride yet this very night."

"I... Is this true?"

"Sir, I ask for your blessing as your daughter is the only woman I have ever laid hands on, and the only woman I could ever desire," John declared before the gathering audience, causing Sarah to blush.

"Is this what you want?"

Sarah stepped forward and took her father's hands, "I can't explain it Daddy. I never thought such a man would want me, and yet... I've never been so happy."

"Then my blessing you shall have."

"And to truly make this evening special, I grant you the Great Tent for the night," Jannine declared, smiling from ear to ear. 'That will show my brother.'

"My lady. Such an honor," John looked as if his eyes would pop out of his head then he turned to his would-be-bride. "Did you hear that?"

"We get a big tent?"

"Not just a big tent, the Great Tent. Tonight, you shall sleep on the royal furs!" he grabbed her and twirled her around in the air. She squealed with delight before running to the girls when he put her down.

"John."

"Yes my Lady" His face beamed with joy.

"You have never known a woman at all have you?"

"No my Lady, why?" (Still beaming...)

"You must go and speak with your Lords. You have much to learn before tonight if you are to hurt her as little as possible."

He went flush, and Jannine had to grab his cold wet clammy hands to pull him into the Village House. Meanwhile, the other men on the ship roared with laughter.

All through dinner, Selrach, Rewdan, and Garth, had John by the ear. Never once could she grasp a single word they spoke for it was often too hushed for any but him to hear. Never-the-less, by the time the feast came to an end and the royal party, plus two, finally began to walk to what would be their camp, John had a look of confidence about him.

"Sarah, come walk with me."

"Yes Jannine. What is on your mind?"

"Have you spoken with anybody yet?"

"Actually, my grandmother told me not to worry. She said if I closed my eyes, he would do what he needed and it would be over to quickly to bother worrying about," she said.

"Sarah, I say this as encouragement." After a quick glance around, she lowered her voice and switched to Cliff Tongue as she continued. "He has been hanging on every word that my man and brothers have had to say all evening. I doubt it will be over quickly at all," Jannine whispered, still looking straight forward as they walked down the coastal road.

"What do mean? Will he.... What is the word? Oh yes. 'Ravage' me?"

"If you are lucky, YES."

"Oh Jannine, do not say such things!"

Jannine took her by the arm and spoke softly in her ear as they walked behind the men still giving her man advice, "Let me tell you a little of what happened on my first night."

"Oh please do Jannine, for I have no idea what to expect."

"When Selrach came to me, he sat before me and spoke of what he thought towards me. He then told me, that as his bride, he had something for me. I asked him if it would hurt bad enough to make me bleed and he said yes. Then he told me that he hoped I would not feel so much pain. I was very confused and asked him how that could come to pass. He than told me that some woman actually enjoy what their man has to give them. I did not truly believe this to be true, yet I could also not believe that he could tell me such a lie. I decided to have faith in him and trust that he would be gentle. I asked him to guide me so that I might learn and not be so afraid. By the end of the night, I was in some pain, but not so much that I did not wish to please him again. I must confess, I did, and still do, enjoy the time we share alone at night. I only hope that you and John will have the courage and faith in each other to find such joy as ours."

"I will pray for such a day Jannine."

"One more thing Sarah."

"Yes Jannine?"

"If you become afraid, look him in the eyes and you will draw strength from each other. When your body is ready for you to not be afraid, your eyes will close on their own."

"Thank you Jannine"

"Now remember, let him enjoy you, then you might just enjoy him as well."

The two disappeared into the tent and all went quiet. Cirtap had already ordered that his men assemble the rest of the tents at a fair distance away, creating a half circle between the Great Tent and the shore. Jannine and Selrach sat staring at the stars wishing them a happy union all night while several of their men, including their brothers, sat up at the main fire praying for the same thing. A blessing tonight would show good fortune on the rest of the journey.

When morning came, they showed no signs while the rest of the camp ate the morning meal. Finally, Jannine decided it best if she approached to offer them some sort of nourishment other than themselves. She went to the door with a large jug and platter and coughed very loudly.

"My Lady?"

"Are you covered?"

"Yes my Lady."

She walked backwards into the tent and kept her back to them while she put the food on the table. "We were just wondering if your night went as well as we had hoped."

"Actually Jannine, I hate to disappoint you, but I never closed my eyes."

"What?" cried Jannine

"It is just that, Oh how did you put it? He awoke such a fire within me that I could not resist 'feeding my hunger within.'"

Jannine turned around with a smile on her face, "Oh Sarah, how wonderful! I did not have such a time till Selrach took me to the Lovers' Pool."

Sarah sat on the bed beside John holding a fur over her chest.

"Well my lady, it was quit a challenge to keep her from screaming such as that."

Jannine could see the same glow in Sarah's eyes and remembered how that felt.

"I best leave you the rest of the day then," the Princess said to her new maid.

"We already rolled up the fur."

Jannine turned to look and saw it lying near the door and then back at John, "Your fellow Warriors have been anxiously awaiting such a sign. There shall be several nights of feasting for you as well Sarah."

"What do you mean?"

"John can explain," she said as she grabbed the fur and ducked out of the tent.

A small post and rail had been set in the earth for the horses to be tied. Jannine saw this as a perfectly opportune site and strutted right over. She held the edge of the fur and gave it a fling over. The men instantly stood and stared. Sarah had produced almost as much as she, and the men responded by breaking out in a roar of applause that would only turn to a roar of song, as the men danced by sunlight around a fire.

Jannine stood by her man's side, glowing with pride, "And to think, some people thought I was making trouble!"

Everybody laughed at that, even Cirtap.

"I have to admit Jannine, you surprised me again," said Cirtap.

Two days later, The King arrived with his other son, Hans, who instantly caught sight of the pretty little blond girl. They all gathered to feast every night and reveled at the festival until a phase of the moon had passed. At that time, King Kerill left his son Hans with his daughter, while her man set sail.

Jannine stood on the dock for the longest of times. Cirtap and Rewdan were both taking a trade ship each while Selrach took the massive Raiders ship with a crew of Plainsman to lead the way. Garth went as second man to Selrach, Primo as second for Cirtap, and Rewdan trailed behind.

"I shall count the phases till your return dear brothers. Your furs will be waiting!" Jannine yelled as they caught their first strong gust of wind.

"Jannine, what do you mean by 'furs will be waiting,'" asked Hans.

"Dear brother, have you never heard of how the Cliff Dwellers offer proof?"

"Would you think less of me if I had not?"

"No"

"Good, because I have no clue what you are talking about," said Hans.

He was as mighty a man as can be grown on the plains. He, too, had hair faded by the sun while his bare chest was already darkly burnt by the first sun of spring. It was clear to all within sight that he was a child of the earth who rode the wind every day that he was not working the soil.

"While we are speaking alone, I could not help but notice a certain someone within the village."

"Her name is Chloris, and as Sarah tells me, she is as pure as I was when chosen for a bride," said Jannine.

"Whoa there little sister, who said anything about taking her as a bride?"

"I did!" Jannine looked at her brother very sternly and said, "No man, not even you, shall count himself welcome in my house if they even think of touching a worthy young woman of my village without granting her due respect. Besides, she is perfect for you."

"How do you know? You never met me before the festival," defended Hans.

"Mother showed me all I need to know. Besides, she thinks so too!"

"Don't tell me you are enduring mother's craft as well?" said an exasperated Hans.

"What do you mean by 'as well'?" inquired Jannine.

"Our dear brother who travels abroad has mother's gift of sight. That is how we knew you had tried to help the man bearing her cloak, and how we knew his mother kept you healing by sleep in her tent," said Hans. "Father never hesitated to believe every word that came out of Garth's mouth when it came to you. Even about the Pools of Life. I, however, did not believe a word till I met a trapper on the edge of the Dark Forest whom spoke of the purest bride having been taken by the Cliffmen's Prince." He stopped and looked at the sky. "Well I thought to myself, 'here is mud in your eye.' It was as if both mothers were punishing me for doubting because I got stuck in blizzard after blizzard only to reach home in time to see your herder Will off."

"I am glad to see they made it before the festival came to an end," said Jannine.

"Exactly how much knowledge has been granted you by our mother?" asked Hans.

"That peace will come when all six of my brothers are happily wedded to six pure brides!"

About the Author
Jamie E. Laleff

Jamie E Laleff was born and raised by English immigrants in southern California. Having traditional parents, she always longed to learn as much as she could about all the diverse cultures around her. The older she got, the more she read while dreaming of traveling all over the world. In 2003, as a wife and mother of three, she decided it was time to start writing something of her own.

Though she has yet to travel all over the world, she has managed to cover much of the continental U.S. Now a full time college student and single mother, she reads to her children and writes for her friends. While dreaming of the day when her family will travel together, exploring the most exotic reaches of our world.